Dead Again
Sequel to Dead & Dead For Real

The United States has been devastated by a two-pronged attack that killed millions. With limited resources, the Union cannot be preserved and California has been taken over by gangs setting up a new nation. Crack U. S. Army sniper Katherine Russell (Kiki) and Nick Sabino battle these forces until the US government is able to return and take over the west coast again. A huge bounty is placed on her head because of her success as a sniper, and Kiki must take out the leader organizing rival gangs to form the new nation of Kalifornia. During an attempt to kill him, she is wounded and rescued by a group of refugee kids. Kiki, along with Nick and the children escape to Arizona for her recuperation. The kids are trained as guerilla unit to return to Los Angeles in the battle against these gangs. Unable to kill Kiki, the gangs mount a raid into Arizona to take out Kiki and her family. They seem to be successful and return to their new nation of Kalifornia, The young guerrilla unit returns to Kalifornia to disrupt the unification movement and prepare for invasion by United States.

By R. L. Clayton

The Evolution River Series
Sea Species
The Envoy
Genesis

Wings of the WASP

The Dead Series
Dead & Dead For Real
Dead Reckoning

Visit R. L. Clayton's websites
www.rlclaytonbooks.com
www.evolutionriver.com

I wish to thank the Tall Grass Editing Co Op for all of the assistance they have given me in taking raw scribbling and making a readable story. It took a lot of patience. Special thanks to fellow authors and editors Melinda Rucker Haynes, Ted Dreisinger, Larry Castriotta and Tammy Atchely. Also, thanks to my copy editor, DeeAnna Galbraith.

DEAD AGAIN

R. L. CLAYTON

DEAD AGAIN

Sequel to Dead & Dead For Real

Prologue

Katherine "Kiki" Russell placed her crosshairs on the bearded figure standing at the dais. His black leather vest was adorned with chains and silver studs, his chest heavily tattooed. In his case, his scraggly beard was an improvement as it covered up more of the scars on his ugly face. He was a secondary target. Sean Gallen hadn't appeared yet.

The silenced .22 would give her time for three or four shots before anybody on the stage understood what was happening, but the low power cartridge meant all the shots had to be headshots. Her plan was extremely dangerous. She was inside the arena, high up in the rafters, and her escape was through a hatch in the roof. Her blind was a gutted air conditioning system, complete with a battery operated motor to keep it humming and vibrating during any search for the assassin, something sure to follow this assault.

Kiki's partner Nick Sabino would fire shots through a glass door as a diversion. He had no targets on the stage. He was four-hundred yards away from her position with her prized 25-06. He had a clear escape route. When things settled down after the manhunt, she would use the Snake Eyes Low Level paraglider system to fly from the top of the six-story dome to their egress point. Four days ago, she and Nick, disguised as facilities repairmen, had moved their equipment in. Nick left, she stayed hidden within the *A/C* unit. She had stashed her SELL paraglider on the roof the night before last.

On the stage were the warlords of the new country, Kalifornia Republik. Sean Gallen was trying to unite them with himself as leader. He was trying to pull the remnants of war-torn California, a land devastated by disease, riots and power outages, together. If he succeeded, it was possible Idaho, Wyoming and Montana would seek to join. A cheer erupted from the crowd.

At a doorway to the side of the stage, a man entered with a dog. He started toward the metal stairway below her, climbing up to the catwalks. No Sean. She could wait no longer. "Go, Nick," she whispered. Kiki squeezed off her first shot as

Nick's shot smashed the glass. The speaker's right eye disappeared. He slumped. One of the other warlords seated behind him jumped up to assist. Kiki ignored him. With the clamor of rising confusion, she could get in more shots. Screams filled the arena. People scrambled for cover. Kiki sighted on a figure huddled behind a chair on the stage. He collapsed. Another of Nick's shots crashed through the glass door.

Below, figures raced up the stairs, guns waving. Brave but foolish, she thought. Kiki ignored them. One man jumped up, yelling for the guards to "Get that cabrón son of a bitch."

Nick fired again. Kiki put a bullet in the screaming man's left eye.

"They're streaming out into the parking lot," Nick's voice came over her com unit. "I got enough time for one more shot."

"Take it. This will be my last one too," Kiki murmured. Damn! Sean Gallen was tall and thin with blond hair. He hadn't been on stage. Was he even here? A giant of a man with an art gallery of tattoos on his bare torso was directing others in the chaos. She put a shot through his ear as Nick's last shot rang out.

The man with the dog raced up the aisle to the front door. Kiki closed the firing-slot. Nothing to do but wait now – maybe more than a day. In the total darkness, she relaxed in the fetal position – all the room allowed in the a/c box. She sipped water sparingly. Too much water and she'd be testing her astronaut diapers.

During the chaos of the Bio-Cyber war, outlaw motorcycle gangs, drug gangs and ethnic gangs had taken over, waging open warfare against law enforcement, the military and each other. As the United States didn't have the resources to fight the insurgents in two wars a continent apart, the decision was made to focus on the eastern United States, and let the gangs and warlords take over California temporarily. Kiki was part of the original U. S. Army effort to retake the state, but got pulled back. She was out of the war and safe in Casa Grande, Arizona. Then she found out Sean Gallen, leader of the Charon's Children outlaw motorcycle gang, had put a price on her head. She couldn't wait for him to find her and endanger those around her.

"I'm away," came Nick's whisper through her com. "I'll let you know when things have calmed down. Sleep tight."

Yeah, Kiki thought. As if. Footfalls vibrated the catwalk beside her box. She tensed, holding the silenced pistol to her chest. If her hidey-hole was discovered, she'd have to shoot her way out. Chances of that succeeding were remote.

She heard the searcher move away. The darkness within her metal cocoon was timeless.

Chapter One

Nick slipped the rifle into the scabbard on his modified trail bike, kicked it into life and took off with a roar. "Outta here," he whispered into the com unit. The cutout on the muffler system assured it would be heard. He zoomed down Hope South to Grand Avenue, under I-10 to Washington Blvd, under I-110 and up the ramp onto the freeway. He needed to move fast, but not completely lose pursuit. That wasn't a great problem, as abandoned and burned out cars choked the highway at places. Passage in a car would be impossible, but the extended suspension of his bike allowed him to weave through the obstacles, stepping over trash, car parts and bundles he cared not to identify.

The last trip he'd made on this freeway was with the U. S. Army. They had a deuce-and-a-half with a blade on the front and bulldozed wrecks off the road, clearing it for the troop carriers. The days and nights of army forays ended months ago. They'd left the city to the gangs. The cleared cars had been replaced with new hulks as people tried to flee this nightmare.

Nick's radio had scanned and picked up the gang's frequency. The ambush was expected. He figured they'd set up before the major confluence of I-10 and I-605, ten miles ahead. The roar of his bike echoed off the faces of the empty buildings. They would have no problem telling where he was. He heard listeners along his route calling in his progress.

Two miles from the intersection, he slowed at an exit before a heavily blocked section of the highway. Nick closed the cutout, forcing the bike's exhaust through an oversized muffler. As he coasted up the ramp, the bike was nearly silent. Moving south through a burned-out neighborhood, he motored away, putting distance between himself and the eastern route. The buildings were abandoned, the streets empty. Darkness had fallen, and he drove with night vision, another shadow among shadows. After five miles, he turned north, surprising a pack of feral dogs feeding on something in a heap of rags. Scattering at his approach, they snarled through bared teeth as he passed. It was twelve miles back to the Convention Center and Kiki.

From the roof of the AT&T building, Nick looked through his binoculars at the Community Center. Throughout the trip back, his radio picked up the growing frustration of the searchers when they could find no trace of him. He'd stashed the bike and worked his way closer. Now to wait for Kiki to escape. It could be hours, maybe a day or more. She had taught him the sniper's talent for patience.

Chapter Two

"Sean, we got somebody scattin' down the freeway on a bike. Might be our shooter," said Max Bolger, Sean Gallen's number two. "I got some hounds chasin' the hare. He ain't movin' that fast. We'll get him."

"Radio ahead," said Sean. "Set up spike strips. I want this guy alive."

"On it," said Max, lifting the radio to his lips.

Sean Gallen nodded and surveyed the mess in the main hall of the Convention Center. His summit meeting had turned to shit. It was a disaster. Four high-ranking warlords killed, several soldiers trampled in the rush for cover or trying to get outside at the shooter. They'd found nothing. He kicked a chair across the stage.

Max Bolger backed away. Max was huge, easily over 300 pounds, not much of it fat. Sean was dangerous when in a mood like this. He would strike without thought. Anyone within range was at risk.

"Goddammit, Max, it took me six months to get everyone to agree to meet. Shit! If Dougie wasn't dead," he pointed at the giant with blood pooled beneath his ear, "they'd blame me for a setup. Some of them are anyway." He waved a hand at the bloodstained stage. "We're building a nation here!" He held his hands out, palms up. "You think any of these lamebrains know that?"

"Whoever it was may have been after you. Good thing you were late," Max offered.

"Whoever it was, was a hell of a shot. Look at this mess. Everyone shot in the head. I knew someone in the Sandbox like this. Katherine Russell. That bitch could do this. The ragheads put a price on her head. I tried to set up a trap and collect, but she escaped. The ragheads called her The *Iblis*. It means Devil. When she came out here with the army, I offered $20,000 for her head six-months ago. She disappeared. Looks like she's back. Max, get the word out that we're offering $50,000 for her head, $75,000 if she's alive."

They walked across the stage to the first victim, the bearded man in the vest. His right eye socket yawned, a gaping hole. His other eye stared at the black ceiling far overhead. "Gus was bringing the northern gangs into the fold. He had a real battle bringing them together." Sean shook his head. "It took me three months to get him here."

The Asian man sprawled behind a chair had a tiny third eye in his forehead. Only a few drops of blood spattered the floor and his black silk suit. "Wang was bringing in San Francisco and central L.A. He was shipping in the workers to get the Imperial Valley going."

"The kids we're picking up from the streets do that," said Max.

"Yeah, but just when we start to get good work from them, they die. The older ones give up or rebel and get shot. The chinks are better."

He pointed to Miguel Sanchez. "The Mexicans will want revenge. We'll have to convince them we didn't do this."

Max's radio squawked. He put it to his ear. "Shit! Set up a perimeter. Close the area and go house-to-house. Find him."

"What do you mean you lost him?" shouted Sean. "How could you lose him?"

Max shrugged his massive shoulders. "One minute our listeners heard him on the freeway. The next it was quiet. We sent guys back, searched the area for signs, set up a perimeter. We're doing a building-to-building search now. We think he went to ground. Nobody heard or saw him leave. We'll get him, Sean."

"Goddam right you will!" Sean shouted. "We can't let some yahoo shoot up our summit. It makes us look bad, in addition to upsetting potential allies. We have to have heads on the flagpoles outside."

Max stood still during the torrent, keeping his face impassive. He had to get Sean off this. "Boss, there had to be more than one shooter," he said, studying the stage and the carnage. The shots from outside were high power. That shooter couldn't see the stage. Headshots by that rifle and these guys wouldn't have heads. And he was shooting through glass. There had to be another shooter inside the building." He slowly looked around the arena. "May still be here."

Sean's eyes grew wide, his head on a swivel. "Let's get out of here, go back to the office. I gotta make calls to see if I can pull this together again. Surround this place so even the rats can't get through. Double-team every door. Use Klieg lights and make it brighter than day outside. I want this sealed tighter than a duck's asshole, and that's watertight. Put a team together. Search by twos. Bring in the dogs. Go through this place top to bottom."

Chapter Three

The arena was a trap. Kiki had to get out. The dogs would find her for sure. When she and Nick built this blind, they had put in a small periscope. It looked like a pipe fitting on the outside. In the cramped box, she had to move like a contortionist to get her head to the eyepiece. Cautiously, she peered through it. There was a man between her and the ladder to the roof. He turned away, looking down at the floor.

Kiki crawled silently through the hatch on the side opposite from the man. Crouching behind the box, she rested the silenced pistol on top and sighted on the man's head. She waited for him to move away from the railing. If she shot him there, he'd topple over, alerting those below. To the side of the pistol was a cloth bag to catch the ejected brass so it wouldn't fall through the grating. She waited like the predator she was.

At last, the man turned and reached for his pocket. She had to shoot before he had anything in his hands. Kiki pulled the trigger, the gun gave a soft pffft. With no drama, the man dropped and lay still. Only murmurs of conversation came from the floor.

Kiki gathered her things into her backpack and holstered her gun in the chest rig. It left her hands free for climbing the ladder to the roof, but was accessible. In her black suit, she would be invisible against the black ceiling.

As she passed the still form lying on the grating, his radio crackled to life. "Gonzo, you there?" Kiki picked up the radio and belched into it. "Gonzo, you motherfucker."

She turned the volume to low and pocketed it. It might come in handy. At the top of the ladder, Kiki noiselessly opened the hatch. She had oiled the hinges earlier.

The night was cool, stars peeking out from behind the clouds. Before the war, light from the city would have reflected from the clouds, brightening the sky and obscuring the stars. Not anymore. Power was still spotty, the city mostly dark. The exception was the area surrounding the convention center. The glare from it was harsh. Withdrawing a padlock from her backpack, she locked the hatch. No surprises. The rumble of the generator powering the lights would mask any noise of her passage.

Beneath the radio tower Kiki retrieved her Snake Eyes Low Level paraglider. She walked to the edge of the roof and set up the mortar-like tube. It would be close whether the wing would carry her past the empty parking lot. If she landed there, she'd be toast.

Kiki strapped on the harness. With one last look around, she pulled the trigger cord. With a soft whump, the black streamer shot from the tube and inflated into the wing-like Para foil. One quick step and she raised her knees and settled into the harness.

The roof slipped away beneath her as a puff of wind picked her up. The extra few feet of height would get her past the glare of the lights. As she cleared the edge of the building, she could see the continuous line of sentries. Oh, Lord don't let them look up, she prayed.

Gonzo's radio gave a soft squawk. Shit! She dare not release the controls to reach for it. They will discover his body in minutes. She urged the paraglider to go faster. A shout arose behind her. As her chute crossed the fence to the executive parking lot, shots whistled by. Shit! She was an easy target. Pico Street passed below, no more than twenty feet. An empty lot loomed. If she could make that, there was cover.

Something hit her leg. The burning started. She'd been shot! She dumped air before the freeway and tried to cushion her landing with her good leg. It buckled. In the tangle of shrouds, she fell forward. Her head smacked the pavement and blackness overtook her.

Chapter Four

Nick heard the shots. Oh, shit! Not good. Desperately, he used his night vision binoculars to search for Kiki. It was like looking for shadows in the dark. He thought he caught a glimpse but couldn't be sure. The shots stopped.

Nick dashed down the stairs and into the street. Dodging from burned-out building to building, he ran toward where he thought he'd seen Kiki. Shouts of other searchers brought him up short. He crept forward. Flashlights glinted ahead. The group of men split up, some heading toward him, others going down the alley. They hadn't found her yet.

Nick ran down a parallel street toward a freeway overpass. Kiki had to have gone that way. He dodged around abandoned cars and heaps of trash clogging the street. At the end was an entrance ramp onto the freeway. It was empty. Cars from an era long gone were dead on the freeway. He peeked around the building toward the alley. Nothing moved. Shouts came from the search party as checked the buildings lining the alley. No Kiki.

Nick had to leave or get caught between the searchers in the alley and those behind him. He chose to run through the underpass to the other side of the freeway. More trash littered the street, burned out cars, overturned trashcans. A wheelchair lying on its side under the freeway, certainly from the hospital, gave him a pang. Perhaps someone trying to escape the ruin that now passed for civilization in Los Angeles.

Shouts and lights behind drove him onward. Where could Kiki have gone? She had to be ahead. The roar of motorcycles behind meant they were moving outward to set up a cordon. He had to get out before the net closed. Nick went left, away from the arena and the search area. He entered an industrial area. A mile further was another underpass.

Crossing under the freeway, Nick moved back toward basement where they had hidden their own motorcycles. If Kiki got away, she'd head back to that point. He dialed through the frequencies used by the gangs until he found the one the searchers were using. They hadn't found her. Dogs entered the search. He could hear the baying through the radio.

Shouting voices told him Kiki's track started and ended in the empty lot where the dogs found and lost the scent. How had she done that? There was no sign of her, no chute, no gear, nothing. The dogs had her in only one spot, where the chute had carried her. He heard several yelps as the frustration of the handlers was taken out on the dogs. They were going back through the buildings. She had to be there.

Nick listened for what seemed like hours as the search turned up nothing. He smiled to himself. She'd foxed them. But where was she? Cautiously he called on the com unit. "K, are you out there? K, are you alright?" Nick didn't want to keep talking on the unit in case the gangs were monitoring their frequency.

His com hissed. No reply, empty air.

Chapter Five

Awareness came to Kiki like dawn on a cloudy day. She took stock. Her head was killing her, a throbbing pain from her forehead. Her left leg burned, her right leg a sharp stabbing pain. Shit, what a mess. She opened her eyes, at least she thought she did. All she saw was blackness. Cautiously, she moved her hand in front of her eyes. On top of everything else, was she blind? Kiki groaned.

"Shhh," came a soft voice. "If the Cs hear us, we'll all be dead, or worse."

Kiki's sucked in air, mouth open. "Where am I?" she whispered.

"A safe place as long as you shut up," came another voice from the dark. The sharp tone was young, like a girl's. Kiki lay quietly, controlling her pain, wondering where she was. She was sleepy. A small voice told her to stay awake.

Later – minutes, hours – she didn't know, she heard the scratch of a match. The soft glow of a candle cast a dim light. Thank God she wasn't blind.

"They've gone." The face of a girl who looked to be eight leaned close. Kiki felt gentle hands on her right leg.

"I've got the bleeding stopped. The bullet went straight through." This voice was older.

She raised her head. Her vision swam as she saw the shadowy face of a boy near her legs. He looked to be about fourteen. She groaned and lay back.

"Lay still. You hit your head pretty hard."

"Who are you?" she slurred out.

"I'm Joel. Who are you?"

"Are you Bat-woman?" asked a much younger voice. "It was really cool the way you flew in there, dressed all in black."

"OJ, be quiet," said another voice near her shoulder. Kiki slowly turned her head. Another girl, about the same age as Joel sat near her shoulder. "She's not Bat-woman. I'm Tammy A but I like

Tama. That's OJ. On your other side is Shalene. Who are you?"

Kiki tried to look around the room, or was it a cave? It smelled earthy. Her eyes refused to focus. These were kids, kids who had saved her life. "I'm Kiki."

"Okay, Kiki, why were the Cs trying to shoot you?" asked Tama.

"Uh, I killed a few of them." The vision of the bodies sprawled on the stage rose in her mind. She smiled into the darkness.

"I knew it! You are Bat-woman!" exclaimed the young boy.

"Hush, OJ," said Tama.

"I'm someone who hates the gangs. Why do you call them Cs?"

"It's the Charon's Children gang who run things here."

Charon's Children, thought Kiki. That name sounds familiar. Her sluggish mind clicked. I know them. Suddenly the name Sean Gallen jumped out. She and Nick had interrogated Andros Gallen during a terrorist investigation three years ago. He was the leader of Charon's Children in Salt Lake

City. They'd disappeared him. "I know them," she said. "Who are you?"

"We're just some kids, trying to keep from getting picked up, trying to survive," said Joel.

"No parents, no adults?" asked Kiki.

"Died of the plague," said Tama.

"Or killed by the Cs," whispered Shalene.

"Wait a minute," exclaimed Joel. "There's a reward out for Kiki Russell. Are you her?"

Should she admit it? She needed a relationship with her rescuers or they could turn her in. "Yeah. You're not going to turn me in, are you?"

"Holy shit!" exclaimed OJ, his wide eyes aglow in the candlelight. "Shit no. We hate the Cs."

"OJ, watch your language," said Tama sharply.

"Where are we?" asked Kiki.

"It's a hideout we use when we're scavenging," said Joel. "The garbage from the C's headquarters has food."

The image of the kids rooting through a garbage bin like rats floated up in Kiki's mind.

"Tomorrow, if things cool down, we'll move to our house," said Tama.

"I can't walk. How will you move me? You can't carry me."

"We can take care of that," said Joel. "I'm more worried about your wounds. When I played football, one kid got a concussion. His eyes didn't focus and he had a bad headache. Does that fit you?"

Oh shit, thought Kiki. That's all I need.

"Your med kit had some antibiotics, so I hope I've got any infection from your bullet wound taken care of for now, but your broken leg is something else. While you were out, I could feel the bones."

"Who are you? Dougie Howser?" asked Kiki. She was met by blank stares. Okay, maybe too long ago, she thought.

"I was in the Boy Scouts, got a couple of merit badges in first aid. I worked a summer job at a hospital as an aide."

"Well, good job," said Kiki. "If I can contact my partner, he's a medic."

"Contact?" asked Tama, "How?"

"My com unit," said Kiki.

"Yeah, we found that, but I don't think it'll work here. We also found a Cs' radio. Doesn't work in here," said Tama.

"You got some neat guns," exclaimed OJ.

"Yeah, be careful. Probably best if you don't touch them." Kiki yawned. Don't fall asleep, she admonished herself.

"Nobody but the Cs have guns here," said OJ in a soft voice.

"We all need some rest," said Joel. "If we travel tomorrow, it'll be a long trip. Can we have some of your rations? We haven't had much to eat today."

"Sure," said Kiki. "I could use a drink. Got any water?"

OJ handed her a plastic milk jug. The water had a slight chlorine taste. Good, she thought. At least it was purified. She lay back, listening to the hushed whispers of the kids. The candle went out.

Chapter Six

"Max, since you're standing in front of me with no heads or bodies, you haven't found them," sneered Sean. He turned and looked out the window of the office he'd taken over.

Max had expected this response. Sean could be nasty when things didn't go his way. "Boss, we're still searching. It's a big area, not a lot of people living there. None of them saw anything."

"They're all lying pieces of shit." He pounded on his desk. "Light up a couple to show we're serious."

"We did that, but I think the shooters are outside our perimeter." Max shifted his weight nervously from foot to foot.

Sean eyed him carefully. Max was one of his best guys. If he couldn't find them, nobody else could. "What did we find here in the arena besides Gonzo's body?"

"The shooter in the arena had a blind disguised as an electrical box. He must have been in there for days. We found food wrappers, water bottles and baggies full of shit. This guy wasn't very big either. It was tight quarters."

"Maybe it wasn't a guy," murmured Sean.

Max looked at Sean for a moment. "Yeah, possible. We had to cut through the hatch to the roof with a torch. He'd locked it with a padlock. On the roof was some kind of mortar tube. We're not sure what that was, but this guy jumped off the roof with a parachute that got him to an overgrown lot where he disappeared."

A chill crept up Sean's back. Was the he a she, Katherine Russell? "Alright, we gotta make it look like we got them. Go down to Watts and pick up a couple of shitheads. Bring them back and smear some of that shit on them. Make a show of the dogs going wild over them. We'll hang their heads from the flagpoles outside."

"Got it, Boss. Meanwhile, we'll quietly keep looking. These guys pissed me off. Nobody gets away with attacking us," Max snarled.

"Yeah. They'll be back, so I want them before we set up a new summit. Bring in the Mexicans and the Chinks to watch the beheading of the assholes. We need a new location, too. It's gotta be one we can secure. We gotta unite Kalifornia before the Feds get any breathing room from the East Coast. A pact has to be in place with them while we're strong."

"Roger that, Boss."

"Max, next week I'm going back to the northern gangs, make sure they got Silicone Valley under control. That's too much income for us to lose. Sometimes those nerds think for themselves. Since Dougie got shot, you're in charge here while I'm gone. Keep the Imperial Valley in line. If they need more workers, take some out of San Diego. We left them alone for a while, so there should be plenty of able bodies to do farm work. Take that bank president we captured. He's still alive, isn't he?" Max nodded. "Take him and his family to Brawley. He's going to open up the First National Bank of Kalifornia. We gotta have a bank if we're going to buy and sell. Make clear it's the only bank. Use the carrot and the stick. Give him a nice house and office. Any fuckups and we start killing his kids."

"What about the ports, Boss?"

"We still getting trouble from the dockworkers?"

Max nodded.

"Kill the union president. Make a statement. You get any objection, kill the VP, too."

"Yeah, but with the quarantine, we're not shipping much out. We got a lotta food stacking up on the docks."

"People gotta eat. Get transport into Arizona and Nevada. Ship east from there. Doesn't matter what we sell it for. Anything is better than nothing. We gotta get the Imperial Valley going, pulling in money. Kalifornia needs income from exports, mostly food and tech. Give the food away if needed. We want to get them as customers. Use our First National Bank of Kalifornia for our transactions until we get more set up. We're building a nation. There's a lot to do."

"Yeah, Boss. We still got our hunter-killer guys out looking for any resistance, but they're not finding much."

"Yeah, the government and the cops left while they could, leaving the sheep behind for us. If most of them hadn't died, things would be hard to handle. It's not like Utah where everybody had guns. We just gotta keep the business brains working for us. They might like it without the government yoke."

Chapter Seven

"Kiki, there's still a lot going on outside. We can't leave yet," whispered Tama.

Kiki opened her eyes. The single candle cast shadows on the dirt walls. "I need to use my com link to tell my partner I'm alive."

"It's dark outside, so we'll move you to the entrance. You should be able to get a signal out, but it has to be short," said Joel.

Kiki looked at the slight shadowy figure. He was not imposing. The girl, Tammy appeared thin also and straight hair hid her face most of the time. In the dim light, she was a silhouette. The small girl, Shalene huddled in the shadow, almost invisible. OJ was beside her, hovering. His ethnic background impossible to discern, but his short curly hair bespoke some African American blood.

"Yeah, I got that. Give me an idea of where we'll be going. I want to let him know so he can stay within com range."

Tama and Joel looked at each other. "Can you code it?" asked Joel.

"Yeah."

"We'll be five miles northwest. That's all I'll tell you for now."

Kiki nodded.

Joel blew out the candle. He and Tama lifted Kiki by the arms while OJ and Shalene picked up her knees. The pain was intense, but she didn't cry out. Shalene put Kiki's broken leg down gently. She pushed aside a curtain. After the pitch-black of the cave, Kiki was able to see in the dimness of the night outside. They moved her through the doorway to a cement ledge.

Close overhead, concrete beams pressed down on her. They were beneath the freeway where a hollow had been dug into the earth of the underpass. The fresh air smelled good after the closeness of the cave. Kiki took a deep breath. Joel put her com set in her hand.

Kiki turned it on, noting the green flash indicating a charged battery. She clicked the send button several times. She whispered, "Nick, two eight five by five, twelve by 2 plus. Twelve twelve F three IJ." She repeated the message then listened until she heard clicks and turned off the com unit.

"That's all?" asked Joel, taking the set from her.

"Yeah, he got it."

"How could he even get the message? It was so short."

"His com will record it logged with the time. I told him in twelve hours we'd be going northwest about five miles. I'll try to call him again in twelve hours on our third alternative frequency. I also told him I was injured. It was a simple code, and if the Cs picked it up, they might break it."

"Wow, you got all that in that message?" asked Tama.

"Yeah. My question is how are you going to move me? You can't carry me five miles."

"The same way we got you here," said Joel. He pointed to the wheelchair lying on its side below them.

***

Nick awoke to the soft chime of his com unit. With ear buds, he listened to the message. Kiki was alive! Relief flooded him. Her brief message said she could not talk longer, but would be moving tomorrow. She was injured, and she'd contact him again. Five miles distant meant he'd have to move. That was out of range for their com units. Okay, he got it. Her injuries still allowed her to travel. The question was did anybody else hear it?

Through his night vision, Nick peeked over the roof edge. There seemed to be no change in the gang compound. He did a survey. The search teams had disappeared, but he spotted a binocular-wielding sentry in an observation post. They'd backed off on the search but were still looking. He'd have to be careful.

To the northwest he saw darkness. Wherever Kiki was going, it looked like wilderness.

Chapter Eight

The administrator's office was now Sean's, with nicely paneled walls and thick carpet. "So somebody sent a message?" The skinny kid in front of him trembled. "I...I think so. It was just numbers and letters, didn't say anything."

"And of course you didn't record it?" The kid shook his head. "Wrote it down?" sneered Sean.

Again, the kid shook his head. Sean spun away.

"Boss, it could be nothing," said Max holding his hands up.

Sean glared at him. "If it was nothing, why did somebody send it?" He pointed at a monitor showing the arena stage where a guy pushed a mop around the floor, wringing it out in a bucket of red liquid. "Can we afford to believe it was nothing?"

Max shrugged. "Maybe somebody was just babbling."

"Yeah, right. On a radio? Max, you gotta be better than this. You," he glared at the quaking kid, "write down what you remember. Let's see if we can make any sense of it. Now!" He pointed at the desk.

The kid dropped into a chair, grabbing a pencil and tablet. He closed his eyes, squeezing them as if to squeeze out what his ears had heard. He started scribbling. He looked up, wrote some more and pushed the tablet tentatively away.

Sean snatched it. "Rick, 28 y wifi 12 y 2 & 12 12 F 3 IJ" he read off. "This is what you heard?"

The kid nodded.

"You sure or you just think so?" Sean snapped.

"I'm pretty sure. The voice said it two times." He squirmed like a boy needing the bathroom.

"Don't go anywhere, kid." Sean turned toward Max. "Help me out on this. With codes, two heads are better than one."

Max shuffled closer. They bent over, shoulder to shoulder.

Max raised up shaking his head after five minutes. "Shit, Boss, it's nothing. It don't make sense."

Sean pointed. "Nah, look at it a little at a time. Rick is the contact name. We got any Ricks?"

"Yeah, I think so. You know everybody changes their names."

"Check 'em out." Sean pointed again. "We got wifi in this city?"

Max looked at the ceiling. "Yeah, there's some places still have that."

"So if that's wifi, then this person is using a computer or phone connection. Twenty-eighty could be referring to an address. The rest could be an email address, I don't know." He smiled at Max. "That's just guesses. What we do know is that there's more than one of 'em and they are not together."

He turned toward the kid. "You, pinhead, go get on that radio. They're gonna talk again," He looked at Max. "Something's going to happen."

The kid got up to leave, his knees shaking, but relief on his face that he was getting away from Sean.

"Hey kid," called Sean.

Putting a hand on the doorway, he turned back.

"What did the voice sound like?"

"It was a whisper."

Chapter Nine

The roar of motorcycles woke Nick. Cautiously, he peeked over the short wall around of the roof of the hospital. Ten choppers surrounded a pickup with two bound figures in the back. What's this? he wondered.

The two men were dragged inside. Something was up. Bikes began to fill the lot, coming in from all directions. In the confusion of this, he could move northwest. Taking a last look from the roof, Nick mapped out a route without much traffic.

He cleaned up, leaving no trace, another sniper lesson picked up from Kiki. In leather vest and black helmet, he glanced at the dust-covered lump that hid Kiki's bike in the basement where they had stored their gear. "Hope we come back to get it," he prayed. "Clear enough," he whispered, peeking out. He motored through the freeway underpass and split off to the residential streets. It would be slow travel, but safer. Five miles west, he turned north. The burned rubble lining the streets had once been homes. The spikes reaching toward the sky had been trees.

These ruins seemed endless. All of Koreatown was ashes.

A five-story office building loomed ahead. Most of the windows were broken and smoke trails stained the outside. That would do. Nick watched from various points around the building for another two hours, assuring himself it was deserted. With the bike on silent mode, he quickly crossed the distance to the service dock. The dark interior reeked of smoke. He hid the bike with his gear in a utility closet and moved to the stairwell. Tiptoeing up the stairs, he paused at each floor to listen. No life anywhere. Cautiously, Nick opened the hatch to the roof.

The rooftop showed the signs of the fire, blackened areas, bubbled roofing. He would have to be careful. As the tallest building in the area, his chances of being spotted were small. Unrolling the solar panel, he set up to charge the batteries in the com unit. It was at least four hours before Kiki would try to contact him again. Naps at any opportunity was the soldier's mantra. Nick set the com unit to the third option frequency and settled in.

The alarm on his com unit awakened him. "Nick, D minus one, A four." Nick clicked the talk button three times to tell her he got the message. He played the recording, listening again. Unbroken darkness settled around him. He needed to move east and north about a mile to approach the destination given by Kiki in her last message.

Nick put on his night-vision to survey the area. In the green glow were empty streets and alleys, buildings with black holes for doors and windows. He watched for an hour before packing his gear and going back downstairs.

Astride the bike in soundless mode, he slid along the streets like a panther on the prowl. The housing changed, becoming more affluent. Some houses looked almost lived-in, showing little damage. All were dark. Had the whole neighborhood packed up and left, closing the doors behind them?

Ahead was a large building, a school, Nick saw as he approached. It was abandoned, like the homes. He stopped at a Mormon temple, hid his bike and settled in to wait.

Chapter Ten

The two quivering men knelt in front of Sean. He looked around the packed arena. "We know you shot our delegates. We found the rifles."

"NO! We didn't do that. You have the wrong guys. We didn't do anything!" The bloody man tried to rise but was beaten back to the floor.

"You say you didn't do it, but we have things you left behind." He held up a baggie. "Our dogs know the scent well. Let's see if they recognize it on you," he yelled, turning to the crowd and holding up his arms. A roar arose.

Two hounds on leashes leapt onto the stage. Their handler strained to hold them back as they yelped, pulling him forward. He lost his grip on one leash. The snarling dog bounded forward, stopped inches from the man. The man froze.

"It seems like he knows you," exclaimed Sean, again turning to the audience. "What should we do with them?" Shouts and yells rose until his ears hurt. "It looks like the jury of your peers says death. You should feel proud that you're going to be key to making a statement. 'Don't FUCK with the Charon's Children'." The rumble of the crowd rose to a crescendo. "Take them out to the parking lot."

Bodies flooded the exits trying to get out. The two men were dragged through a service entrance. One screamed, thrashing, fighting his captors. The other was silent, his legs unmoving, feet scraping across the floor.

Outside, the afternoon sun made slanted shadows across the parking lot. The rowdy crowd parted as the two men were hauled to a plastic bin at the foot of the flagpoles. "I'm tired of listening to this one blubber," said Sean pointing to the struggling man. "We'll do him first."

The man was forced to his knees. One biker sat on the back of his legs, pinning them to the concrete. Another grabbed the man's hair and pulled his head over the bin. "The more you struggle, the worse this is gonna be," said the one holding his hair. "It'll happen no matter what you do."

"I didn't do nuthin," whined the man. "Nuthin," he screamed.

Sean moved near the bin. He raised a Samurai sword above his head. With a yell, he slashed down. The man's scream stopped instantly. The biker holding the hair fell backward with the head in his lap. Blood shot from the neck splashing into the bin. A wall of noise went up from the crowd.

The other man was dragged forward and stretched across the bin. Again, Sean's sword flashed downward. The two heads were attached to the ropes of two of the flagpoles and hoisted up. Another roar from the crowd. Sean dipped his finger into the blood and smeared a streak across his cheeks. With the sword held aloft, he re-entered the arena.

"That'll keep them quiet for a while," Sean said to Max. "How's our search going? Anything?"

"We got people on the radios listening for any messages and observation posts checking for any movement. We'll pick up something."

Sean took a large swig from a bottle of tequila. He handed the bottle to Max. "Let's look at that message again," said Sean, picking up the scribbles. He stared at it. *Rick, 28 y wifi 12 y 2 & 12 12 F 3 IJ.* "Max, read this aloud to me."

"Rick, twenty-eight y wifi twelve y two & twelve twelve F three IJ," Max read.

"Slur the words," said Sean. Max read again. "Do it in a whisper." Max read it. There was something but Sean couldn't quite get it. He took another swig of tequila. "Let's get something to eat. I'm starving." The message wiggled around in his brain. It was the key to finding this *Iblis*.

Chapter Eleven

The kids struggled to move Kiki from the cave. Under the darkening sky of early evening, Joel and Tama took her shoulders while OJ and Shalene took her knees. They eased her out onto the ledge above the road and below the freeway. The pain was horrible, yet Kiki couldn't call out. The kids slid her down the face of the underpass and placed her in the wheelchair. Most of her gear was in a backpack on the back of the chair. Kiki was shrouded in a dark blanket, her silenced pistol hidden in her lap under the bag of scavenged food.

Kiki soon lost track of their route as they zigzagged through alleys and deserted buildings. With hushed voices in the gloom, they sought to put distance between the arena and themselves. OJ and Shalene hung close, watching the gaping windows and doorways in the abandoned buildings for danger.

"Where you kids going?" asked a gruff voice from behind.

They all jumped. "We're taking my grandma away from here," said Tama over her shoulder. Joel kept pushing the wheelchair, kept them moving.

"All of you stop right there. Honey, let's have a look at you."

"Leave us alone," said Joel. They turned. In the dwindling light, the man was dressed in black, a silhouette looming large.

"Back off, pipsqueak." The man reached into his waistband, pulled a pistol and held it up for them to see. "Let's not do anything foolish, eh?"

Kiki moaned, trying to make her voice sound old and cracked. Fighting the wheels, she turned the wheelchair to face the man. Face hidden under the blanket, she moaned again.

"Shut up, Grandma. I oughtta kill you now. We got no use for old leeches anymore." He gestured with the gun. "Step over here, babe. You," he pointed the gun at the rest, "all stay quiet over there and I might let you live." He leaned close to Tama, inhaling deeply. "Nice." He turned back to the others. "You three take Grandma outta here. This one," he looked at Tama, "will join you later, maybe."

There was no sound of a shot, only the snick-snick of the action on Kiki's pistol cycling another round into the chamber. She didn't need a second shot as the man dropped to the ground with a splat like a sack of wet mud. The stunned kids stared, frozen with eyes wide and mouths open.

"Strip him," directed Kiki. "Take anything we can use. Drag the body over behind that dumpster."

"Holy shit!" exclaimed OJ. "You shot him. I didn't hear anything."

"Quiet," admonished Kiki. "We don't need more company. Go help." The man was heavy. They struggled getting his clothes off. It took all four of them to drag the body toward the side of the alley.

"This guy really stinks," whispered OJ, holding the pants at arm's length. "He shit his pants."

"Sometimes happens when you die," said Kiki. "Hurry up. We need to get out of here."

"Lemme push her," said OJ as he moved behind the wheelchair.

Tama and Shalene strode ahead, Joel walked with OJ and Kiki. He reached over to help push the wheelchair. "I can do it," OJ admonished.

"How did you shoot that guy?" he asked. "There was no sound."

"Good," said Kiki. "Special gun." She groaned as the wheelchair hit some bumps.

"Sorry," said OJ. He slowed slightly. 'One shot in the head! Wow, what shooting! Can you teach me to do that?"

"OJ, I hope you never have to do that. Taking somebody's life can't be undone. You take a life you can't give it back."

"Yeah," he said quietly. "The Cs killed my dad, made me watch. I couldn't give his life back."

"I'm sorry, OJ," Kiki whispered. She shivered thinking what these kids had been through.

"We'll be there in about an hour," said Joel.

Kiki turned on her com unit. "Nick, minus 1."

OJ pushed faster.

"I need to give my partner a site or address so he can meet us," said Kiki to Joel, looking up at him.

Joel was silent. "There's a Mormon temple near where we're going. The tower is the tallest thing around. We could meet him there."

Kiki thought. "Nick, alpha n, twelve five nineteen two fourteen four and thirteen one fourteen eight one twenty twenty one fourteen. Ack." Three clicks sounded in her headset.

"Joel, I need to stop. I'm bleeding again."

OJ stopped the wheelchair, gave a soft whistle. Tama and Shalene returned.

"Push me into that doorway so we're out of the street," Kiki directed, her voice weak.

Using Kiki's shaded flashlight, Joel looked at the bandage over the bullet wound in her calf. It was sopping with blood. "I'm going to have to redress this. It'll take a little time. OJ, push her inside. Tama, OJ, you keep a watch. Shalene let's drape this blanket over us. You hold the light."

Under the tent of the blanket, Joel raised Kiki's leg. She was unable to suppress a moan from the pain. He removed the soaked bandage, poured antiseptic into the oozing hole and onto the new bandage. He wrapped the bandages, trying to get compression on the wound to stem the flow of blood. Kiki moaned at the pressure.

"Sorry. It's the best I can do for now. We'll do more at the house."

Kiki fought off a curtain of blackness as they resumed the trek.

Chapter Twelve

Nick couldn't be so lucky as to be at the destination already. The alpha numeric for twelve five nineteen was LDS and the rest signified the corner of Second and Manhattan. The Mormon church. It wasn't much of a code, anybody with knowledge of the area would figure it out, but the range of the gang's radios didn't extend this far from their headquarters.

Since his arrival two hours ago at the Outpost Estates, he'd been watching. Nothing had moved. Leaving the bike and his gear behind, Nick slipped from shadow to shadow toward the house/church. He pushed the door open and the reek of death assaulted him. Makeshift beds filled the large room. Bodies lay everywhere. In the green glow of his night vision, a few rats scurried away.

What had happened here? Some of the bodies were obvious smallpox victims, but most had been shot. A table against one wall was overturned. Empty packets labeled *Vaccine, Smallpox* littered the floor. Covering his nose to block out the stench, Nick entered another room, a supply room. More gunshot victims lay against one wall. They'd been lined up and executed. The rats had been at them.

More vaccine cartons lay on the floor – all empty. This church had been set up as a vaccination center, but somebody had attacked it, killed everybody and taken the vaccine. Nick continued his search of the temple. The place had been ransacked. Nothing of value remained. He had to get out. Fear of disease wasn't the reason, it was the vision of devastation.

Taking in lungfuls of fresh air, Nick sat in a shadow to the side of the door. God! What a mess. The visions of what happened inside froze his mind. The sound of gravel crunching pulled him out of the nightmare. Down the street, some kids pushed a shrouded figure in a wheelchair. Totally still, Nick watched them approach. It had to be

Kiki, but caution kept him from rushing out to meet them.

Nick clicked his com three times. The shrouded figure moved. "I'm at the door," he said. Kiki said something and the kids pushed faster. Nick emerged from his hiding place and moved to the wheelchair. "I'm here, K."

"She's hurt pretty bad," said the small boy who had been pushing.

"We need to get off the street," said Nick. "Where can we go so I can check her out?"

The small boy began pushing Kiki toward a group of houses a few blocks away. Nick hurried to keep up, the kids ran ahead as if fleeing a monster.

The house they approached was shuttered behind an imposing wall. Though dark, it looked undamaged. At the rear, they approached a heavy gate. The older boy took a key from his pocket unlocked the gate and pulled it open. Nick helped the small boy push Kiki in. The gate closed behind them. They wheeled her around a covered swimming pool to the back door of the house.

It was unlocked and they entered the stygian blackness. The door closed with a click. Matches scratched and flared. Several candles sprang to life.

In the dim glow, Nick glanced around at the kitchen. It was spacious, with tiled walls. A large island with granite countertops dominated the floor. The gas stove and a double oven filled one wall. A double-door refrigerator and floor to ceiling cabinets filled another. The windows had been covered by cardboard with duct tape.

At the wheelchair, Nick peeled back the blanket shrouding Kiki. Her face was gray, her eyelids fluttered open. Shit, she needs a hospital, thought Nick. He wheeled her to a table. "Help me get her on the table," he said to the kids. They all gathered around her. "Spread that blanket on the floor," he directed. "We're going to ease her onto the blanket, then we'll lift her onto the table."

Kiki moaned as they slid her from the chair onto the blanket. With the kids all lifting, they moved Kiki onto the table. Nick handed the older boy a candle and began his examination.

She was cold–loss of blood, he feared. Her broken leg needed to be set. Nick unwrapped the bandages from the other leg. "Did you dress this?" he asked the older boy. He nodded. "What's your name?"

"Joel."

"You've done a good job, Joel. Did you have some training?"

"I was a Boy Scout."

"You learned well." He looked at the other kids. "What are your names?"

The girl of about seventeen stepped forward. "I'm Tammy A, but I'm called Tama." She pointed to the younger girl. "Shalene, and that's OJ."

"Thank you for saving her," Nick said. "She really needs a hospital, but we'll have to do what we can to help her."

Joel spoke up. "In the basement of the temple are supplies that the raiders missed. There's medical stuff there."

"You've been inside?" asked Nick. They all nodded. "What happened?"

"The Cs came in, shot up the place and stole the vaccine," said Tama. "They did that all over the city."

"How did you escape?" asked Nick.

"We heard 'em coming," said Tama. "They herded all the kids together and shot all the adults, but we," she looked at the others, "managed to hide in the basement. They brought in trucks to haul off everything, including the other kids. We don't know what happened to them. They just left the bodies and the sick." She fought off tears. OJ and Shalene couldn't. Silent tears leaked from their eyes. "The Cs haven't been back since.

"Joel, take me back to the church. I need to get supplies."

Wearing his night-vision goggles, Nick checked the street from the front door. It was empty. He followed Joel back to the church. They masked their faces, spreading menthol gel from Kiki's first aid kit on their noses to block the smell. Joel led Nick through the carnage to a bathroom. In the back, he unlocked a door. They descended the stairway into the inky blackness of the basement.

Nick removed his night vision glasses and turned on a flashlight. Cabinets lined the walls. Leave it up to the Mormons to stock supplies for years. In addition to medical supplies, shelves of food filled the room. Bless them, thought Nick.

Everything he needed was there. This church was an emergency hospital, but they hadn't counted on a ruthless attack. After loading bags with supplies, Nick and Joel locked the door, picked their way through the room upstairs and headed back to the house and Kiki.

Chapter Thirteen

Kiki was stretched out on the padded island, candles on both sides held by OJ and Shalene. She got her first good look at the kids. Joel stood at the head of the table. He had sandy hair and his face showed teenage acne. His soft brown eyes were full of concern for her at the moment.

Tama stood to one side. She was slender with long straight dark hair, matted and tangled. Her eyes were brown, her face taut with concern. Kiki looked to the other side.

OJ rested a hand on her shoulder. "You'll be okay," he said. He was short, and his curly black hair bespoke of mixed heritage. She smiled up at him.

"With your help I will." Kiki tried to grip his hand, but her arm refused to move.

Shalene stood near her knee, her head barely above the countertop. Her corn-silk hair was dirty and knotted, her child's face smeared with grime. "Please get better," she said.

Kiki's nod was almost impossible to see.

Nick swabbed her leg with alcohol. "K, I'm giving you a sedative. We have to set your leg. Even with this anesthetic," he held up a syringe, "it's going to hurt a lot." He injected the local. Kiki nodded. "Joel, take her hands, grip the wrists. Tama, you hold her knee. Sit on it."

Kiki looked steadily into Nick's eyes. He tapped her leg. "Feel that?" She shook her head. Nick put a rolled washrag in her mouth. "Scream if you have to."

Nick grabbed her ankle and pulled. With his left hand, he felt the bones move as he attempted to align them.

The pain was unimaginable. Kiki's mind became a blinding flash of agony. A scream built trying to erupt. She refused to let it go, funneling it into a growing black ball. As long as she held that ball away from her, didn't let it touch her, she had control. If it enveloped her, she would be lost to it, something she wouldn't allow.

It stopped. Eyes squeezed shut, from a distance Nick instructed the kids to help put a cast on her leg. She opened her eyes. The candles seemed so bright. Everybody huddled at the foot of the table. The ball of pain grew and shrank as they moved her leg. It stopped again. She saw tears on Nick's cheeks.

"I'm sorry, Babe. I'm so sorry. I'm going to give you more sedative so you can rest."

The heaviness took her.

"Roll up blankets and put them on each side," Nick instructed. "Put that rolled towel under her knees. She should be out for twelve hours. We'll keep watch."

With Kiki secured, Nick turned to Joel. "Thanks for getting her away. How did you find her?"

"We heard the Cs shooting at her," said Joel.

"She came out of the sky!" exclaimed OJ. "I thought she was Batman, flying and being all in black and stuff."

"Anybody the Cs are shooting at might be our friend," said Tama, her face grim. "I think she broke her leg when she landed."

"We had an old wheelchair we got from the hospital, use it when we scavenge," explained OJ. "We gathered her batwings and stuff and wheeled her to the cave before the Cs found us."

"A cave, huh," said Nick. "Where is this cave?"

"The homeless dug it under the freeway at the overpass," said Joel. "Nobody uses it now except us."

"No wonder I couldn't find you," said Nick "I was there just as the gang arrived. Had to leave. You guys pushed her all the way from there?"

"We had to wait until things cooled off," said Tama. "We heard guys passing by. The Cs were looking for her real hard."

"Yeah, and that radio is pretty neat," exclaimed OJ.

In a quiet voice, Shalene said, "We ran into a C on the way. He was going to keep Tama. Kiki killed him." Her face wore a troubled look.

Tama wrapped her in a hug. "It's okay, baby. It's something that had to be done. He was a bad man."

"Nobody else was there," said Joel. "We took his stuff. Kiki said it might be useful."

"Where is he now?" asked Nick.

"We stashed him behind a dumpster," said Joel.

"It's been several hours since, right?" asked Nick. Joel nodded. "So that's probably about three miles."

"Yeah, about two hours before we got here."

"They'll miss him soon, if not already," mumbled Nick.

Joel handed Nick a walkie-talkie. He turned it over in his hands. Not his, must belong to the Cs. He turned it on. A faint voice came through the static. They were at the extreme range of the radio. "Anybody heard from Jax?" a voice crackled. "He hasn't checked in." There was silence. "Guys, hold your positions. We're gonna send out somebody to check on him. Stay on the air."

"We're going to have company," said Nick. "Know somewhere we can hide? It's has to be close so we can move Kiki."

Shalene took Nick's hand and led him into the back yard. Joel and Tama followed. OJ stayed with Kiki. They walked around the swimming pool to a tool shed. Inside, Shalene shined a flashlight in one corner. Joel moved some yard tools aside to reveal a disguised trapdoor. "It's an old bomb shelter," said Joel. "It's where we stayed when the Cs came the last time."

Shelves of supplies lined the walls – some canned food, water, first aid supplies, batteries. On one wall were bunk-beds, doubles, space to sleep eight people. Nick turned toward a locker with a padlock in one corner.

"We don't have a key," said Joel.

In another corner was a sink and toilet. A table had been pushed into another corner. Electronic equipment – a radio, monitors for surveillance cameras outside covered the top.

"The solar panels on the house roof power things down here," said Joel.

"Did you know about this before all the trouble?" asked Nick.

Tama nodded. "I lived next door. Sarah was my best friend. Sarah's family was kinda survivalist, not extreme like on TV, but when things got bad, they left for a cabin near Big Bear." She looked at Joel and OJ.

"When the plague broke out, all the Mormon families went to the temple," said OJ. "We went, too and got vaccinated. They stayed in the temple but we came back to our families. The Cs killed everybody in the temple, then spread out in the neighborhoods and took everybody prisoner or killed them. I was hiding. They found me and made me watch as they killed my family. Then I broke away and ran."

Nick shook his head. What a terrible thing for kids to go through. "There's food here. Why were you scavenging?"

"We'd need that if we had to hole up for a long time," said Joel.

Nick nodded. "Let's get Kiki down here and cover our tracks. I don't know how long we'll have to stay."

"Last time, it was a week," said Shalene, her voice soft.

Chapter Fourteen

"Boss," said Max, leaning against the doorjamb in Sean's office, "Jax ain't answering his check-in. I'm gonna send some guys out to see what's what."

Sean Gallen looked up from behind his desk. "Where's his post?" he asked.

"Jax said he was setting up about three miles northwest, on the south side of Koreatown."

Sean looked out the window at the darkened city beyond. "Max, read that radio message to me again."

Max picked up the paper and moved closer to the lantern light. "Rick, twenty-eight y wifi twelve y two and twelve twelve F three I J"

"Lemme see it," said Sean, holding out his hand. I'm gonna read it different. You listen." Max nodded. "Rick, two eight y y fi, one two y two and one two one two F three I J."

"Boss, that sounds different. Let me read it like that."

Sean handed him the paper.

Max put his hand over his mouth, slurring and muffling the words. "Rick, two eight fi y fi. One two y two."

"Hold it, Max. Okay, the first is a name like Rick. That we got. The second part sounds like a heading two eight five. That's where Jax was, right?"

"Yeah about three miles away. Two eight five by five, maybe?" said Max.

"You got it, Max. They're on a heading of two eight five and five miles out! Send out the troops. We'll get them." Max hurried out. Sean looked again at the message. F three was probably a communication frequency. The rest was probably times to send more messages. IJ might be injury. They'd find out soon enough.

Sean put on the black leather vest showing the years of wear and the prominent banner of Charon's Children, a grinning skull in the flames of hell. It was his club *cut*. He grabbed an AR-15 and a .45, checked they were loaded and headed out to his bike.

Max had gathered twelve guys similarly clad. They milled near their parked bikes under the flag poles. Above the group hung the two heads of the shooters, flies thickly covering them. The odor of death wafted in the air, blood splatters stained the concrete below.

"Jax hasn't called in from his post," Sean looked from face to face. "We need to go check it out. If something happened to him, it may be someone who helped these scumbags." He pointed up. "These assholes killed our people and shot up our summit meeting. Nobody attacks us and gets away with it. Be ready, they got guns and know how to use 'em. I want 'em alive. We gotta find out who they're working with."

Sean straddled his bike, slid the rifle into the scabbard above his handlebars, and hit the starter button. The bike came to life with the familiar *potato-potato* rumble of a Harley. It idled for a few minutes. "Max, keep things going here. I'll let you know what we find."

Whoever these shooters were, they had put a serious dent in his efforts to unite California into his new nation, Kalifornia. His creditability had taken a hit. Without looking back, he roared through the deserted streets, headlights stabbing into the darkness, heading for the 101. Jax had set up his post south of Koreatown.

Chapter Fifteen

Nick and the kids gathered around Kiki. "We'll all pick her up together and carry her into the shelter. Joel, you and I will come back to make sure this house looks abandoned. Ready? On three."

Getting Kiki down the stairs was tough. She moaned in her sleep, but it had to be done. They laid her in one of the lower bunks. Nick and Joel returned to the house.

"Joel, park this wheelchair in the garage, like they left it there. Grab the bags of stuff. I need to go hide my bike."

"Nick, do we need to take this bag?" asked Joel holding up the trash bag with the bikers things. "It really stinks."

Nick pulled out the clothes. The jeans were bad. He emptied the pockets. Nothing special about them. He held up the biker's *cut,* the grinning skull in the flames of hell painted on the black leather vest. Charon's Children was emblazoned across the top, below it said Salt Lake City. Nick froze. Shit! The pieces started falling into place.

"What's wrong?" asked Joel.

"I'll tell you later. Let's get this place cleaned. Nothing we can do about the smell of the candles except hope it's gone by the time they get here. I'll see you downstairs in a few minutes."

Nick hurried out to where he'd stashed his bike. He moved it into the school, finding a janitor's closet big enough to hold it. He covered it with rags and a mop, then tipped a set of shelves over on it. That should satisfy the casual eyes. Grabbing the duffle bag of gear, he headed back. The whole time his mind turned over the idea they'd run into the Charon's Children from Salt Lake City again. And Sean Gallen had to be related to Andros Gallen, the gang leader they interrogated.

Joel was waiting for him when he got back to the shelter. Nick nodded that things were okay. Joel arranged the camouflage to make the entrance look like a tool board on the wall in the storage shed.

A single LED light lit the shelter. Nick saw that Kiki was asleep. OJ sat at her side. Tama and Shalene placed some military style meal-ready-to-eat packages on the fold-down table.

"Thanks," said Nick, realizing how hungry he was. They ate in silence. He set his soup aside for Kiki. "I pretty much understand how you kids got here. Are there other groups you know of?"

Tama nodded. "We've run into other groups. Some with grownups, others were just kids, like us. The groups are four or five people, nothing bigger. We're all just scavenging to stay alive and hiding out from the Cs."

"What happened to our world?" asked Joel, his eyes pleading. "One day everything seemed normal, and within weeks people were dying everywhere and nobody had electricity. It all went dark."

"The United States was attacked," said Nick. "It was a two-part attack. The first part was a bio-attack with smallpox, a disease we had little resistance to. Millions died before we were able to make a vaccine." Nick looked down at the table and shook his head. "The other part was a cyber-attack. Our electrical grid was disabled. Most of the big cities were hit hard. The government tried to use the military to maintain control, but it wasn't enough. California was lost to the gangs," he said in a raspy voice.

"What about you and Kiki? What are you doing here?" asked OJ.

"Kiki and I came to LA with the military soon after the attacks, to fight the gangs. We're ex-military. Kiki was a sniper in Afghanistan. She was good, very good. After the Arabs murdered her family, she came back to hunt them down. We got them." Nick's smile was grim.

"She was good against the gangs here in LA, too. They put a price on her head high enough to buy loyalty. We had to leave. After the government left California to the gangs, we asked to come back to LA and do what damage we could. We're doing damage."

"She's still got a bounty on her head," said Joel. "We heard it on the radio."

"Yeah, but it's just the two of us. Nobody buys our loyalty and only two or three others know about us."

"You got us, too," said Shalene quietly.

Nick smiled. "I do, and thank you for saving Kiki. We're going to have to get her back to a hospital as soon as the coast is clear."

"How are we going to do that?" asked Joel.

"We have to get near Point Mugu. Camp Pendleton will get a chopper to pick us up."

"And then what?" came Shalene's soft voice. "What happens to us?" A tear rolled down her cheek.

Chapter Sixteen

"Jax said he was here," stated Sean, pointing at the burned out storefronts. "Spread out. Search in twos, building-by-building. We're looking for anything. Make noise. If he fell asleep and his radio is busted, that's the best thing we could find." Sean revved his bike. His followers rumbled away, the roars echoing along the empty streets.

Sean glanced around. The burned-out and deserted buildings were silent, yet he felt an aura. Something happened here. He sensed it like a lingering odor. The word **Iblis** rose unbidden in his mind. A chill crawled up his spine. Did Katherine Russell know he set up an ambush to have her killed in the Sandbox? Was this personal or business? He tried to follow her movements after she returned to the United States. She had hunted down the killers of her family and destroyed the terrorist cell. Then he lost her. His inquiries and searches came up empty. She disappeared, only to turn up here in Los Angles three years later. Maybe.

"Boss, we got something!" his radio crackled.

"Where are you?" Sean inquired.

"Two blocks north. We found his bike."

Sean arrived within one minute. The bike sat inside a smashed grocery store. Nothing seemed wrong with it. No sign of Jax. "Fan out. He's here somewhere." More searchers arrived going from building to building. "You men take the alleys," he directed. If Jax were asleep or doped out, Sean would kick his ass.

He walked to the bike. The keys were in the ignition. Jax wouldn't leave it like that unless he was close. What happened here? Sure, Jax had a problem with girls, but there was no sign of....

"We found him, Boss. We're in the alley behind the store," crackled a voice over his radio.

Sean hurried through the building, kicking out the broken back door. Guys were gathered around the dumpster. He shouldered his way through them. A naked body lay crammed between the wall and the rusted metal. On his back was the club ink. He saw no blood.

"Pull him out." Two men grabbed his legs and dragged him into the alley, laying him on his back. His eyes stared into the black sky as if seeking stars, a small neat hole in his forehead. She had been here! Was she still lurking nearby waiting for him? His mind froze. He glanced up at the surrounding rooftops.

A gust of wind swirled trash down the alley. Sean scowled at the men around him. "Scour this alley for any sign. Our killer came this way. Watch your asses." The men spread out by twos looking at the ground, nervously watching the gaping windows.

Sean picked up his radio. "Hey, Max. You there?"

"Yeah, Boss."

"We found him. Shot in the head, small caliber bullet. It's the same shooter from the arena. I think it's Katherine Russell. She took his clothes and left his bike."

"How's she traveling, Boss?"

"We're looking for signs now."

"Why'd she do Jax? If she'd left him alone, we'd have no clue where she was."

"Yeah," mused Sean aloud. Why did she do him? Had he surprised her? She wouldn't have looked like a danger, being small and a woman. She probably looked like a girl in the dark. Yeah, he could see Jax with his guard down and his dick out. Why did she strip him? If she was afoot why not take his bike?

"Think about it, Max." Sean didn't have a ready answer either. "I'll get back to you in a little while."

"You guys find anything?" Sean yelled.

"The wind's screwing up tracks, but I swear no vehicle went this way. 'Course, I'm not an Indian tracker," yelled one guy.

"Looks like some kids and a couple of bicycles went north," yelled another guy. "Only a few tracks, though. Wind erased the rest." Sean walked up the alley to take a look.

The tracks were faint, going only a few feet. It was more of a hint than a clue.

"Max, we got nothing sure. Looks like some kids went this way, but nothing of her or a vehicle."

"Whatcha gonna do, Boss?" came Max's voice through the static.

"We're looking north to see if we can find anything. Things all right there?"

"Yeah, Boss. Under control."

Under control. Sean hoped so. If they didn't find anything, they'd have to go all the way to Ventura and talk to Hijos de Hades. Sure, they were his allies, but he could never fully trust them. ***Iblis.*** Again he looked at the rooftops. His stomach flipped and knotted as he imagined crosshairs centered on his chest.

Chapter Seventeen

Nick looked from the radio to Tama then at the other kids. "We good here?" He gestured at the bomb shelter.

"They searched here before and didn't find us," said Tama.

"We probably have about fifteen-minutes before they arrive," said Nick. "Joel, let's make a last check. I'd like to move a body from the church and drape it near my bike. That will deter them, I hope."

"Yeah, I'll help," said Joel, rising from his chair.

"Tama, do something with the wheelchair. They might put together that those weren't bike tracks."

She nodded. "Right. I'll put it in a closet in the house, throw dust on it."

Nick took a last look through the monitors to be sure nobody was around.

Joel and Nick dashed to the church and grabbed a sheet with a rotting body on it. At the school, they put it half in and half out of the doorway to the janitor's closet. They arrived back at the shelter within minutes.

Nick made a quick check of Kiki. She had a fever. He gave her another shot of antibiotics. The last thing she needed was an infection. Please, K, hang on until we can get you to a hospital, he prayed, giving her a light kiss. Her eyelids fluttered at the touch.

***

In the room lit by a single light, they huddled together watching the monitors, listening to the microphones. The rumble signaled that company had arrived. Six bikes flowed up the street, stopped and the leather-clad men spread out to search through the buildings. The search was quick, not really looking for something as much as hoping their presence would cause someone to move, cause a reaction.

The radio crackled. "Find anything?"

Nick recognized Sean's voice.

"Nah, Boss. Pretty dead up here. Houses are good and stuff, but no people. We hit the church, remember? Lots of bodies there. Everything else is empty. Doesn't look like anything's moved here since then. Maybe he went over the pass or into the mountains."

"Yeah, possible. Keep checking anyway."

"Okay."

Through the front door monitor, Nick and the kids watched the long-haired fireplug of a man enter the house. He exited out the back in five minutes and glanced at the shed under which they sat. He shook his head, beard waggling. In that moment, Nick knew he was done searching their grounds.

Half an hour later, the bikes roared away. Thanks, whoever you are suggesting the idea of the mountains and the pass. They were the diversion he and the kids needed. They let out a collective sigh.

Nick walked over to Kiki. She opened her eyes and gave a weak smile. He put his hand on her forehead. Her fever had risen. This was troubling.

"Joel, we have to get her out, and soon. Know of anything we can use to carry her?"

Tama spoke up. "My family has an ATV. I think it's still in the garage. We can use that."

"Let's eat and you can show me. It'll be safe by then."

Tama nodded and lit the gas burner to heat soup for Kiki. Shalene brought MREs for them. They ate in silence. By the time they finished, Kiki's soup was warm. Nick braced her up and spooned some into her mouth. She swallowed then turned her head away.

"Don't make me force-feed you," he said. She smiled and took a few more spoonfuls. He laid her back as her eyes closed.

Tama's house was locked and untouched by the riots. She pulled a key from under the flowerpot with the dried stick that used to be a plant. Out of habit she disarmed the alarm, though without power its battery was long dead. Through the kitchen, she led Joel and Nick to the garage. A large black SUV sat on one side, a camouflage green Kubota ATV on the other. Tempting though the SUV was, it would not do well in the blocked streets. When off-road, it needed at least a trail to follow.

Nick walked around the ATV. There was room for the driver and one passenger up front. A mattress in the back would work for Kiki. OJ would probably insist on riding with her.

"Not enough seats, huh?" said Joel.

"I'll put Shalene on the back of my bike and you ride with Tama," mused Nick aloud.

"That would work, but I have a trail bike at my house. It's only three blocks away. I could take it."

"Either we have to travel fast or silence the vehicles. My bike has a whisper mode."

"There's an auto parts store in the strip center. We might find what we need there," said Joel. "It's about a mile away."

"Let's go back so I can check on Kiki. You and I can get my bike and go to the store. Tama, pack whatever you think we'll need."

Chapter Eighteen

Yeah, the Bony Mountains Wilderness would be her style, thought Sean. If she and her partner were up there, they could set up an ambush. Take a lot of his guys out before they ever saw her. Maybe even him. Was this whole thing a way to lure him into a trap? Sean had never run from anything, but she scared him.

"Max, you there?" Sean asked into his long-range radio.

"Yeah, Boss."

"We're going to check Laurel Canyon and on toward Ventura, see if they went that way. We'll alert the Mexis to watch for them."

"Be careful, Boss. The Mexis are mad about Sanchez."

"Yeah, we'll tell them these are accomplices we're looking for."

"I hope they believe you."

"Yeah, me too." Sean's bike rumbled to life as he started north, paralleling the freeway on surface streets.

Abandoned vehicles clogged the freeway through Laurel Canyon. Travel was difficult on the once-rapid passages through the urban areas. Homes and buildings didn't show the devastation in other parts of the city, but all were abandoned. The rumble of the bikes echoed down the empty streets. Sean stayed with part of the advance team, sending others to check out the neighborhoods around Koreatown.

Where would she go? he wondered. Did she have outside help? She had at least one partner. Were there more? Was the U. S. helping her? Had that bastard, President Donaldson, lied to him? If they had U. S. support, they could be trying to get to Point Mugu. It was the closest U. S. installation.

The roadblock ahead signaled they were approaching Mexi territory. Hijos de Hades moved into the vacuum left when the government collapsed. Agro areas like Ventura were ripe for takeover because of the immigrant populations.

Four years ago, Hijos and the Cs had a good business relationship when Andros ran Charon's Children in Salt Lake City. Hijos supplied, the C's distributed. Now they vied for control over the new Kalifornia. They had to unite, but under who?

Sean had a dream when he came back from the war in the Mideast. Charon's Children in shambles because his brother, Andros, had disappeared, leaving no one in charge. Sean knocked a few heads, offed some dissidents and took over. When the U. S. government collapsed, he moved. California was wide open, and he grabbed the opportunity. Now he had to hold it together.

He signaled for the bikes to slow at the barricade. Two mustached men with AKs stepped out, blocking their way.

"We need to talk to Sanchez," said Sean.

"So, who are you?" asked the fattest one.

"Tell him Sean Gallen is at his gate and needs to talk to him."

The man walked away, a walkie-talkie stuck to his ear, and returned within five minutes. "He'll be here in an hour. Have a seat." He pointed to the curb.

Walking back to his bike, Sean fumed. He was pissed—pissed that these assassin assholes hadn't been caught, pissed that they had disrupted his plans for Kalifornia, and pissed that he had to wait here. If this shooter was Katherine Russell, he'd really be pissed he hadn't killed her in Afghanistan. He paced.

"Boss, calm down," Sam said. "You can't let them see you sweat." Sam nodded over his shoulder toward the gate. Sean sat on his bike.

Shit. He knew that. This Russell woman was getting under his skin. Sean pulled out his radio. "Max, you there?" No answer. He clamped down on the spike of anger from yet another frustration.

"Boss?" his radio crackled.

"Yeah, Max. We're at the entrance to Ventura, Hijos territory. I gotta let them know there're some assholes out there trying to kill us. I want them working with us."

"How much you gonna tell 'em?"

"Alternative channel two," Sean said as he switched to a seldom used channel. Though not secure, someone would have to know which one was Alt two.

"Max, you there?"

Yeah, Boss.”

“I’m only telling them what I have to. I think both us and Hijos have history with Katherine Russell back when Andros disappeared.”

“Whaaaaat?”

“Yeah, what you don’t know was that there was this sniper in the Sandbox who was hurting the ragheads bad. They put a price on her head, but when our little ambush failed, they contacted Hijos with a contract to kill the sniper’s family. That sniper was Katherine Russell. She came back from Afghanistan and hunted down everybody involved, including the Arabs. Hijos was doing deals with the Arabs, paying us in H to carry out the hits. Then the Hijos chapter in Albuquerque got hit. Andros started getting instruction directly from the Arabs, contract stuff.”

“Yeah, I remember,” said Max. “It was some nasty shit. I didn’t like that much.”

“It was a contract, Max. One day, Andros meets with the Arab. He gets new directions. The Arab disappears, but nobody notices for a while. He never was social, only spoke to Andros. A few days later, Andros disappears, as in forever. Then a lotta shit starts falling on the club.”

"Andros would never rat us out."

"I'm not saying he did, but nothing was ever heard of him. Even the police records had nothing. We don't know what they did to him to make him talk. Under enhanced interrogation, everybody talks eventually."

"Wow, Boss. I never knew most of that. But Andros would hold out for a while. The shit started falling within days."

"Yeah, There's no way to tell what they did to him or if it was him ratting on us. I don't know if he's alive or dead. No one but you and me know this, and soon, Sanchez."

"Yeah, Boss, the Hijos will be on board. They got popped good after Andros disappeared, too. Word was raids in Mexico took out a lot of their operations. You think this Russell bitch was behind that?"

"Behind, I don't know. But I'm sure she was involved."

"This Russell bitch and her partner must have split up, Boss. We tracked the one on the bike east. This one's going north."

"Yeah, possible, but I think the one going east doubled back. My gut's telling me they're up here somewhere, together or not. We'll get Hijos' help and do a proper search. Not even the rats will go unnoticed."

"How are they moving, Boss?"

"Yeah, I'm wondering that, too. The one going north didn't go far. I gotta believe that one's on foot. The other one could have doubled back, he's got wheels. The question is where are they going? Hey, Sanchez just pulled up. Call you back later." He turned to the approaching leader of the Hijos de Hades chapter in California. Sean put on his confident game face, though it came with a struggle. That goddam woman.

Chapter Nineteen

In Joel's garage, Nick gave the muffler clamp a final twist. The normally sleek trail bike was ugly, and any passenger would get their legs burned. He started the engine. It made a soft purr. Revving it, he and turned to Joel. In a natural voice, he said, "This will do." Joel smiled. It was quiet.

Nick had guessed that the Cs' emergency radio channel was their Alt two. He had been stunned by the message. His and Kiki's past were going to bite them. Once Sean informed the Hijos that he and Kiki had been behind their problems three years ago, searchers would flood the area hunting them. They had to get out now! Inside the garage, Kiki was bundled atop a sponge mattress in the back of the Kubota. OJ hovered beside her. Water and MRE's were packed around them. Tama was behind the wheel and Shalene was buckled into the passenger seat. Joel sat astride the bike.

Nick spoke to the kids, "After that radio message, Point Mugu is out. Route One is a choke point. We'll head west on 3rd as long as possible. I want to get into the Westridge Canyonback Wilderness Park. At Crescent Heights, we go north to Sunset, then west to Mandeville Canyon. That'll take us to the wilderness area. We'll find a trail and hide out. I'll arrange for pick up."

Tama and Joel looked at each other. "We've been there," they said in unison.

"I heard there're people in the wilderness who've gone savage," said Tama.

"Yeah, me too," said OJ.

"Okay, we'll be careful. Joel, you take Kiki's radio. I'll scout ahead and keep in contact. You stay with the Kubota, but drop back to check our tail once in a while. Get me on the radio if you see anything." He handed Joel Kiki's silenced rifle. "You know how to use that?"

"Yeah, I went to Arizona for a Boy Scout camp with shooting ranges. They don't allow any of those in California."

"Can you shoot someone?"

"I...I think so, if I have to."

Doubt was written all over Joel's face, but it was the best Nick could hope for. "Keep one in the chamber with the safety on. If something happens, take a breath and do what needs to be done. Clear?"

"Yes, sir."

Nick handed Kiki her silenced pistol. "Okay?" he asked. Her gray face gave a hint of a smile, a single nod. He put his own silenced .22 in the bike scabbard. Kiki's sniper rifle was broken down and tucked in his kit strapped to the back of the bike. He looked back. With speed and luck, they'd find a pick-up spot. He opened the garage door, gunned the bike and moved along 3rd Street in a whisper. Behind came the soft drone of the Kubota and Joel's bike. The street was cluttered with trash, abandoned cars and the occasional heap of cloth that didn't beg further inspection. It was passable as they moved toward the afternoon sun.

With his headset on, he switched to his secure military contact channel, pushed a send button. He heard clicks followed by a buzz. "Interior Secretary Ron Carson here."

"Ron, this is Nick. We're blown and hot. We're heading for the Westridge Canyonback

Wilderness Park. Can you arrange a pickup in about two hours? Put a medic on board, Kiki's bad. We also have four passengers."

"I'm on it. Turn on your beacon so we can find you."

"I'll conference with you when we get to Pendleton. Out." Nick liked that Ron didn't ask any questions. Nick had to stay focused. He switched over to Joel's channel.

"Joel, okay?"

"Yeah, checking our tail. It's clear."

The road was quiet, deserted. Nick set his radio monitor to check for activity on the C's channel and the Alt two channel. The hiss of empty air met his ears. He scouted ahead, but the only signs of life were packs of mongrel dogs and occasional rats. Bits of paper swirled like autumn leaves, disturbed by his hushed movement. As he turned onto Mandeville Canyon Road, he stopped to wait.

The road faded into the shadow of the valley floor as the afternoon sun dipped behind the mountain. He didn't want to call back to Joel on the off chance the Cs were listening. His military channel was secure. The tone buzzed twice before it was picked up.

"Carson," came the answer.

"Ron, this is Nick. We're moving into Mandeville Canyon from the south. Can't get to Point Mugu."

"Yeah, we re-tasked a satellite to take a look. I'm linked in. The Hijos are moving to cover all roads into Mugu. I'm locked onto you. If you'd continued west, I'd have called. The rest of your group is about five minutes away. We have twelve minutes before we lose this view, but another satellite will be in place in an hour."

"Ron, how far to any kind of pick-up site?"

"There's a large building, looks like a church, at the end of the road, about six miles ahead. The parking lot is perfect. If the chopper comes up the valley, we won't be visible from the city. It can set down there."

"Anything else in the canyon?"

"We've been checking with infrared. No heat signatures from any of the houses. It appears everybody got out while they could. On the road in we're seeing warm spots. Someone's there. I show two bodies and a hot spot. Cooking fire. Might be one more in some kind of shelter.”

“Can we bypass them?”

“Doesn’t look like it.”

“I’ll check it out. Call you later.”

“Nick, I’ll let you know if we see something.”

“Thanks, Ron.”

Chapter Twenty

The approach of the Kubota and the bike was nearly silent. Nick did a quick check. Everything seemed good–except Kiki. Sweat beaded her forehead. She was hot. The antibiotics weren't working against this infection, and she was growing worse fast. Her eyes fluttered open. He placed a straw in her mouth.

"You need to drink water." She sipped. "More," he commanded.

"Guys," he turned to the kids. "Our pick up is up the canyon." He pointed and their eyes shifted toward the road disappearing into darkness ahead. "Our help tells me there's someone up there. We'll go slowly. In about a half-mile, we'll move everyone off the road, find a spot. I'll scout ahead."

The canyon was almost dark when they stopped. Nick checked out a house at the end of a driveway just off the road. It was empty. They could stay there while Nick scouted further up the canyon.

Nick took another look at Kiki. "Hang in there, Babe," he whispered. He turned to see the kids watching him intently. "We'll be fine. Watch over her while I see what's ahead."

Nick glided up the road. His NV goggles had an infrared function display overlaying the green of the night vision. A bright spot ahead alerted him.

Stashing the bike, he took Kiki's silenced .22 pistol. Creeping forward, he parted some brush. Ahead, two slight figures, perhaps women were kneeling over a small fire. The house behind them was dark, but Nick suspected someone was inside. He backed away. He needed a plan besides killing those people. He returned to his group.

"Why are they there?" asked Joel. "Are they guarding something or hiding out?"

"That is the question," stated Nick. "I only saw two people, but there was a heat signature inside the building, so probably one more."

"We have to talk to them," said Tama. "I could go. I wouldn't be a threat to them."

"That's risky, T. I don't like it," stated Joel, his arms crossed.

"Yeah, it is risky," agreed Nick. "What if Shalene and I went? Are you okay with that?" he asked.

Tama spoke up, "Joel and I will make sure nothing happens to you."

Shalene said nothing. "Tama," Nick said, "I need you to stay with Kiki. Joel can cover us in case anything happens." Nick looked at Joel. "You could do that, right?"

He nodded.

Tama started to object. "Tama, OJ, take care of her until we get back. Try to get her to drink more water."

"I'll take care of her," OJ said solemnly.

Nick pulled Shalene onto the back of his bike and eased away, Joel following.

Shalene clung to him like a life raft. Both he and Joel wore night vision. The two bikes whispered up the road, easing toward the camp. They stopped four hundred yards away.

"Joel, I'm going to set you up close, but not too close. If there's trouble, you'll have easy shots. Keep the NV goggles on. Shoot only if Shalene or I am threatened. This .22 is silenced, so it won't make noise or have a muzzle flash. We don't want to attract any other attention. I don't know what we're walking into, so you are our safety net."

Nick removed most of his gear, tucking the silenced pistol in the small of his back. He took Shalene's hand and walked toward the small fire and two figures.

"Hello the camp," he said in a voice they would hear. Both figures rose. One cradled something. "May we come in?" They said nothing.

With Shalene in hand, Nick stepped onto the paved driveway and into a dim circle of light. Two women wrapped in blankets faced him. One looked to be in her mid-twenties and strikingly beautiful, black hair, dark eyes over high cheekbones full lips. The other woman was older, suckling a baby. Nick circled so he could watch the women and the doorway to the house at the same time.

"Who are you?" the younger woman asked haltingly, her Spanish accent apparent.

"My daughter and I are trying to get to the church at the end of this road. Our family said they would meet us there," Nick lied. Shalene was behind him, peeking around his leg at the two.

"No one is there," said the woman. "No one has passed us."

"They may not have arrived yet. We need to go there to wait for them."

"You cannot pass," rasped a voice from the doorway. A medium height man stepped into the flickering light. His complexion was dark, his hair black, his body thin. He held an AK-47. At a growl from him the two women scurried to one side, giving him a clear shot at Nick and Shalene.

"We just want to go through," said Nick, holding his left hand out palm up. His right hand stayed at his side.

"Nobody comes up here. Nobody leaves here," said the man, swinging the rifle up toward them. "Sorry señor, wrong place, wrong time."

Now, Joel, Nick thought. Nothing happened. "You can't kill us just for coming here," pled Nick. "We've done nothing to you." He tucked Shalene protectively behind him, his right hand wrapped around the butt of the pistol. Come on, Joel, Nick prayed.

As the man brought the rifle to his shoulder, Nick threw Shalene to one side. He rolled to the other, the pistol out and aimed at the man's head. The snick-snick of the action was the only sound as a small hole appeared in the man's forehead. He toppled backward, the AK clattering on the pavement.

Nick turned toward the women. Their mouths were open in surprise, their hands raised over their heads. The baby suspended in the carry cried out.

"No, don't shoot. We're not part of this."

"Anybody else around?" asked Nick. They shook their heads. "There was only Jesus. Ricardo left this morning to get more supplies from Hijos. He'll be back later."

Nick heard Shalene behind him. She had skinned her elbow when he pushed her out of the line of fire. "Are you okay?" he asked over his shoulder.

"Yes," she answered in a small voice. He looked back. Her gaze was glued to the body. Nick waved toward Joel. Within minutes, he stepped into the soft glow of the fire.

"I couldn't do it, Nick," he wailed. "Sorry, I just couldn't do it." There were tears in his eyes.

"It's okay, Joel. It worked out. I'm glad you didn't. It's something that would haunt you." Nick knew Joel needed some consoling. He could not let guilt eat him up right now.

Nick turned back to the two women. "What's going on here? What are you doing here?"

"My name is Rosalinda Villa. This is my sister, Monica Dalos," she said, gesturing to the other woman. "The baby is Arianna. Jesus and Ricardo were sent up here by Hijos to guard the pass, keep people from entering Ventura through the mountains." She went over to the body and extracted a radio from the leather vest. "They brought us along as toys," she hissed. She spat into the eyes staring at nothing. "Cabrón," she grunted.

"Joel, go get Tama and Kiki. We need to move." Joel turned, his shoulders slumped, a picture of misery. "Be careful, Joel. There might be others they don't know about." The woman started to speak, but Nick raised his hand to silence her.

The baby began to cry. Shalene looked up, eyes round. "Would you like to see my Arianna?" asked Monica, holding the baby out. Shalene nodded and walked toward Monica who sat on an overturned bucket. She pulled back the blanket.

"Rosa, we have to get to the church. What are you going to do?" Nick asked.

"As badly as Ricardo and Jesus treated us, they kept us alive. When Ricardo returns tomorrow, he will find Jesus and radio back to the Hijos. They will tell him to question us then kill us. We cannot run. These houses," she gestured up the valley, "got no more food left. There is not enough life in the mountains. We have nothing to kill or trap animals. I will choose a quick shot over starving," she gestured toward the AK on the ground.

"I have to talk to someone. Stay here." Nick walked out of earshot and called Ron.

"We took care of the roadblock and will proceed to the church. One small problem. There's two more to come with us. They have valuable information about the Hijos. Can we handle it?"

"Anybody weigh as much as you?" asked a new voice.

"Who's that?" asked Nick. "Nobody else was to know about us."

"It's CIA Director David Kennedy. He's providing your transportation. I had to bring him in," said Ron Carson.

"Yeah, Okay. I'm just worried, with the new price on Kiki's head. No, the women are small, about 125 pounds or so, Joel and Tama are both rail thin as are the smaller kids. Kiki's shed weight as she's gotten worse."

"Yeah, the chopper can handle the load. Our satellite will be in range in thirty minutes. Your ride is leaving Pendleton now. He'll orbit off the coast until we give him the signal. You better get moving."

Nick returned to the women as Joel and Tama arrived. "We gotta move. Rosa, Monica, you can come with us. We're getting a ride out of here."

Shalene's face mirrored the smile on the women's faces. "Rosa, you ride with me, Monica and the baby ride in the Kubota." He handed Monica the AK. "Don't shoot anyone." They were overloaded but the trip was short.

As they wound up the dark road, Rosa's held tightly to him. He was doing the right thing, Nick assured himself. Rosa and Monica had useful information about the Hijos they would need when they returned. At least he hoped so. They couldn't run a refugee service. The Hijos represented a second front to be concerned about. If anything, they were more savage than the Cs. The vision of headless corpses hanging from the bridges of Mexico arose.

Chapter Twenty-One

Sean clasped Miguel Sanchez to him in the traditional gang symbol of solidarity. They had moved into a large house not far from the barricade. It was a rich man's house. Sunlight streamed through the large window, played across the wood floors, the paintings on the walls, the posh furniture. "Nice digs."

Sanchez shrugged. "We make do."

"We're after the people who killed your brother."

"You said you caught them," said Sanchez sharply.

"Yeah, but these are the brains behind the shooting. We think it's a man and woman. If it's who I think, we both have some history with them."

Sanchez stared at him, waiting for more.

"When I was in the Sandbox, there was this sniper, Katherine Russell. She was hot. By that I mean highest number of kills in the Middle East. The ragheads put a bounty on her head, dead or alive. I set up an ambush so I could collect. Didn't work out. After that, the Taliban sent a team to Mexico and the U.S. to kill her family. Hijos de Hades was the Mexican side of the contract, Charon's Children the U.S."

"Yeah, I remember something about getting pure H from them for some *asesinatos*," said Sanchez.

"Well, she came back and hunted down the U.S. side and the Arab connections. That was when my brother, Andros, disappeared. Soon after, so did she and her partner. There were no records of them."

"One of our major *jeffes* was snatched." Sanchez rubbed his jaw. "He doesn't talk 'bout how he got away, but he let slip that a man and woman flew him from a boat. They told him he was going to be tortured on that boat."

Sean nodded. "Could be them. Anyway, Russell came back when the army tried to take back Los Angles. I put a price on her head. She disappeared again. Now there's this shooting that takes out four major players in our conference, including your brother. It was sniper work, her style. She's back."

"So, whose heads are on the flagpoles?"

"Just some assholes we picked up. I had to make it look like I was on top of this." Sanchez nodded in agreement. "Last night, someone killed one of my sentries down near Koreatown. Small caliber, head shot. Her signature. We think she's coming north trying to get to Point Mugu."

"Is she connected with the U. S.?" Sanchez asked, his eyes narrowing.

"Maybe, or maybe she's just got some friends there. I know she's got a hard on for me. She saved a lot of American lives in Afghanistan. Her military rep is gold. We need you watch the northern routes for these assholes. Be careful. The woman is dangerous."

"I already got people on the major roads. I'll beef up the roadblocks. I also got people in the mountains. I'll tell them to be alert."

"Thanks, man. I'll let you know about a new summit schedule. If we want to keep what we have, we gotta organize." They hugged again. "Sorry about your brother. Let me know if anything happens." Sean walked through the barricade toward his guys and their bikes.

He didn't trust Sanchez or Hijos. But they needed each other. For now. He picked up his radio. "Max, you there?" Sean asked.

"Yeah, Boss. How'd it go?"

"The Hijos are going to close off the north. We need to bring in more people and start sweeping east and west. They're here somewhere. I feel it. Another thing I want you to start checking. She's with someone, a partner. See if you can find out anything about who it is. Her trail is dead, but she went somewhere when she left LA."

"Yeah, Boss. I'll get someone on that. I'll send fifteen guys to meet you to start the search."

"You got things going in the Imperial Valley?"

"We're working on it, playing nice with the farmers. We'll make sure they're growing."

"Good. And, Max, listen. We need these farmers to like us. We supply workers, we help them get whatever they need to grow, we supply them banking, and our tax rates are lower that California's were. Get some engineers over to the geothermal power plants. I want them up and running."

"We're on it, Boss"

Sean paused, looked around, taking in the mountains, blue sky, the warm sun. He sighed. "Ya know, Max, even with a smaller tax rate, it's more money than we've ever seen before. We need that money to get this country going."

"Got it, Boss."

"Max, have these guys you're sending meet us where Jax was. We'll start the search from there. If I split up into two teams, one going east and the other west, we're sure to find something. They'll be back and it won't be for fun." Sean had a bad feeling. They had to get them. Katherine Russell wouldn't quit until he was in her crosshairs. She didn't miss.

Chapter Twenty-Two

The silence of the valley settled around Nick. He glanced at the small group gathered in the parking lot of the church. Hurry, Ron, he prayed. Kiki had to get to a hospital before the infection ran amok in her system. Nick's radio crackled, making him jump. "Nick, there's a vehicle on the ridge road above you," said Ron. "Our satellite picked him up. He's using lights, so he has no night vision. He'll be above you in about ten minutes."

"We're trying to stash the bikes and the Kubota now. How long until the chopper gets here?"

"Forget the gear," admonished Ron. "We'll have the chopper there in thirty minutes."

"This guy's going to find the body at the roadblock before that," said Nick. "He's going to radio in and start moving up the street toward us. Nobody else can reach us in time to do anything, but he can. I'm going to have to go down and take care of him."

"Yeah. Be careful. Call me from the chopper."

Nick turned toward his small group. Rose and Monica were off to one side with the baby. "Looks like Ricardo is on his way back. He must have gotten some news about us. I'm going to go make sure he doesn't interfere. He'll be on the ridge road above us. Tama, you watch Rose and Monica. If they do anything to alert him, shoot them. Can you do that?"

She glanced at them then at OJ and Shalene. She turned toward him. He looked at her eyes. There was steel there. She nodded. He believed her and handed her the silenced rifle.

"OJ, you and Shalene watch Kiki. Joel, you're with me." They climbed on his bike and glided down the road toward the roadblock. Joel clung tightly to him as they wove down the darkened street.

Nick stopped fifty yards from the blockade camp. After parking the bike behind some scrub oak, he and Joel walked toward the embers of the cooking fire. Jesus lay where he had fallen.

"Nick, I couldn't shoot, I'm sorry. I tried." Joel's voice grew quiet. A sob escaped his lips.

"Joel, when I joined the army, I was a medic. I never wanted to shoot anyone. I wanted to save people." Nick looked away. "But life took me in another direction. I hate it. I don't want to kill anyone, but our world doesn't afford us that luxury anymore. What I'm saying is I understand and I respect you for admitting it. I really hope that doesn't change, because taking a life changes you, and I can't say for the better. Sometimes we don't have a choice. Those we love must come first." In the dim light, Nick could see the torment in Joel's face, tears rolled down his cheeks. He needed support. "You're not a failure, Joel. You're a good kid."

"Thanks, Nick."

"Let's drag Jesus's body out of sight. I want you to stay in here and make some small noises. Ricardo will come to investigate. I want him in the doorway where I have a clear shot. You okay with that?"

"Yeah," came Joel's soft voice.

"Joel, you'll be fine. You can do this. I need you to do this." Nick tried to reassure him before he went back outside and found cover in some brush. It gave him a clear field of fire from the driveway to the door. He built up the fire to give him more light and settled in, assembling the AR-10. The gun would be noisy, but Nick was convinced they were alone and he needed firepower to ensure one shot, one kill.

Joel was a good kid, and Nick regretted that his new life put him here. He wanted to shelter him, and in another era that would work. Not today.

The sound of an ATV roused him from his reverie. He saw the headlights flash as it worked its way down the ridge road to the pavement. It was not silenced, its burr announcing its arrival.

The chubby dark-haired man climbed out of the driver's seat. "Jesus," he called. Nick heard a moan from the house. "You *bastardo*. You fucking again?" He walked toward the open door. "I got some news. Some *asesinados* are on the loose."

Ricardo peered through the open doorway. Nick placed the crosshairs on the back of his head. The gun hardly bucked against his shoulder as the man's head disappeared in the thunderous retort. A quick check and Nick moved toward the house. Joel was curled against the wall covered in brain matter. Nick pulled him up, hugged him. It was like holding a statue.

"We have to go," said Nick. Their chopper would be arriving within minutes. Nick ripped the man's shirt off and wiped Joel's face, removing most of the mess. He pulled Joel outside and put him on the bike.

"Hang onto me." They scooted away from the gruesome scene and up the road. Overhead, was a whir, not loud, but distinctly that of a silenced helicopter. They had to hurry.

Arriving back at the church, Nick saw that the helicopter was already on the ground, idling. Tama had driven the Kubota up to it. She and OJ were struggling to get Kiki aboard. Nick rushed to help. Kiki moaned as they lifted her. "It's okay, Babe. We're getting you to a hospital," Nick whispered in her ear. Her head gave a single nod.

The others scrambled aboard, finding seats, strapping themselves in. The rotors sped up, and the floor lurched beneath them. Nick radioed Ron. "We're aboard."

"Good. I'm coming to Pendleton. I'll see you there." Nick looked at the darkness below, a solitary light, a lonely spot shone, the fire at the barricade with its bodies. Given time, he could have hidden everything and caused more confusion. That beacon below was an arrow pointing at them.

Chapter Twenty-Three

Kiki felt the vibration of the helicopter beneath her. Her mind roamed in the delirium of fever. She was back in the Sandbox. They had received orders to take another village and her vantage point was a hill 600 yards distant. From here she could cover her unit as they advanced to liberate another town. The operation was hurried. Intel said there were Taliban in the town preparing to leave. They wanted to capture or kill them.

She had a clear field of fire for her Barrett 50. With this rifle, she could punch through walls, reach out and put some serious hurt on the enemy. None had poked their heads up yet. She was locked onto the rifle, her eyes peering through the twelve power scope. A yell from Corporal Ling pulled her away. He began firing his M-4.

She looked up. Black clad figures were rising from the brow of the hill. Shit! They were surrounded. This was a trap! "Cap, we need help. We got troops all around us."

"I'm calling in air support. Hang on. We're coming."

Kiki knew her help would never arrive in time. "Dyson, cover the south and east. Ling, cover the north and east. I'll take the west. Place your shots. Help is on the way, but we gotta hold out until they get here."

There was little cover, they were exposed. Kiki lay prone, presenting as small a target as she could. The Barrett 50 was too much gun for close quarter, but the red mush it made of her targets was satisfying. It clicked empty. She grabbed her Beretta. The west was clear, for now. She turned in time to see Ling take a head shot, his helmet keeping his brains from scattering. She fired at two advancing figures, both dropped.

On her other side, Corporal Dyson grunted. Red flooded from his back. She crawled to him. It was a chest shot. If help arrived soon, he might live. She cradled his head and fired at another figure. He jerked backward, arms flailing.

A roar filled her world. Dust stung her eyes. Her shoulder burned. Had she been shot? Her arm didn't work. A soldier was above her. Where had he come from? He said something, but she heard nothing. Behind him another black-clad figure rose. She fired. It dropped. Another rose. She fired again. Her gun clicked empty.

The soldier picked her up and carried her to a helicopter. Where had that come from? He laid her gently inside and he and another soldier turned back toward Dyson. She watched, as if from a great distance. They placed Dyson on a stretcher and carried him to the medevac. Beside her was Ling. How had he gotten there?

The two medics jumped aboard and the floor pressed into her back as the helicopter rose. A face swam before her.

"Are you alright?" he asked.

"How's Dyke?" she asked. He looked away.

"We're working on him."

Her head swam.

There was a jerk. She looked up to see Nick. His eyes were closed. This wasn't the Sandbox. A chill wormed its way through the fever. Oh no. Not the Director. She squeezed her eyes shut to try to block this out. She was too weak to fight off this spirit, this being who had come into Nick's and her lives years ago. It was not of this physical world, and it fed on human emotions. Different emotions were like different flavors to this being. The Director influenced men to violence and hatred because it preferred those emotions. For a reason she didn't understand, it had developed an affinity for her and Nick. She hated it. She felt like a missionary in the pot looking at the cannibals, waiting for it to feed on her.

"Hello Katherine. My, what a mess you are. You have to fight this sickness. I need you. Your world is full of despair, and that sourness is not a flavor I like. You bring such fear and hatred to your enemies, and those are tastes I savor. Nick is languishing in care and concern for you. That part of me that likes the taste of love and caring is feeding on him now. Bah! Buck up, girl. I need you."

Get out of my head. I can't fight you now. Kiki struggled to block the voice in her head.

"Do not fight me. I am not your enemy. Save your strength for the battles ahead. Your enemies plot to find you. Sean Gallen has hatred so strong it burns me when I eat it. Lovely. Coupled with that hatred is his fear of you. You stand between him and his dream of being king of Kalifornia. He knows you are his nemesis. Only you can defeat him. Get well."

Kiki pushed back against the Director with the last of her energy. She lapsed into a feverish panic as the helicopter landed. Hands pulled her onto a stretcher. Blackness descended.

Chapter Twenty-Four
Two Months later

Nick peeked into the hospital room as he knocked on the door. "How you feeling today, K?" he asked.

Kiki glanced out the window at the Catalina Mountains rising in the distance. She had been in Northwest Medical Center in Tucson for a month. "I want out of this place. They keep waking me up to give me sleeping pills. It's full of sick people. If I don't get out soon, I'll really become sick."

Nick laughed. "That's the K I've been looking for. We'll have you out today. How do you feel?" he repeated.

"Not as good as I will when I'm outta here."

Four heads peered around the corner. "Joel, Tama, OJ, Shalene. God I'm glad to see you," exclaimed Kiki. "I never had the chance to thank you for saving my life. Without you dragging me away, the Cs would have me."

OJ stood beside her bed like a guard. She reached over and mussed his hair. "Thanks for taking care of me." He beamed as she gathered the kids to her in a group hug. Looking up at Nick, she said, "Let's go home, Nick."

Kiki was propped up in the front seat of the Suburban. The kids chatted behind her. The desert rolled by as they drove up I-10. The view of the Silverbell Mountains brought memories of her parents, her husband, her daughter that almost stopped her heart. That seemed like a century ago, yet the hurt had lessened only a little. She pressed her lips tightly together, suppressing a sob. How could the world change so much?

There was traffic on the interstate, things were getting back to normal, if that was the right word? What was normal now? They exited onto Interstate 8, and after a short distance, exited again. Within five minutes, they were climbing the twisting driveway to Nick's home overlooking Casa Grande.

The front door opened as they pulled up. Nick's mother Miriam stood, arms open to hug Kiki. "Lordy, girl we've been worried about you. It's wonderful to have you back."

"Glad to be home, Miriam. You look good."

"Thanks. Teaching and kids brought vigor into my life."

Kiki laughed. "Yeah, they did that for me, too."

"Go on out to the patio. I'll bring refreshments. Can you have adult drinks yet?"

Kiki's laugh was good. "Another day or so. Tea will be fine."

"Kids, you want to swim?" They yelled and dashed off to don suits. Nick carried the meager bag of Kiki's things to their bedroom.

From the patio, Kiki surveyed the valley below. Buildings were being constructed, things were moving, the city was alive.

"It looks almost like it was before," said Nick as he approached. His arms went around her. She leaned into him, comfort and security flowing through her. Screams brought her back as the kids ran from the door and plunged into the pool. It was heaven.

Seated at the table, iced tea in front of her, she asked the question that had nagged her for weeks. "Nick, what happened? I don't remember anything after the kids pushed me away from the tunnel. The next thing I knew, I woke up in the hospital."

"You had a massive infection. It almost killed you." He closed his eyes, his head moving side to side. "I thought I'd lost you. I nearly did. The chopper took us to Point Mugu. They were ready with medical staff and filled you full of newly developed antibiotics. That worked, but it took time. Ron was there, so I demanded they fly us back to Tucson."

"What about the kids? They're here."

"I insisted they come with us. Rosa and Monica came too."

"Who are they? I don't remember them at all."

"The Hijos' guards brought them up to the barricade in Mandeville Canyon to keep them company and do the slave work. They're working with Stephen at the restaurant right now. They'll be here in a couple of hours."

"Nick, what happened in LA? Did we do anything besides kill a few bad guys?"

"Sean Gallen is still trying to pull together a coalition, but we set him back. He intends to establish the country of Kalifornia, separate from the U.S."

Kiki frowned. "I know what Gallen wants. So we did delay him. What about the rest of the United States?"

"Recovery is slow. Power is being restored as fast as we can get components. Much of the northeast is still bad. The latest estimates are that we lost more than half of the population to disease, starvation, and the elements. The president has mobilized forces in the rebuilding efforts. They seem to be paying off but it's not moving nearly fast enough."

"Casa Grande looks good," noted Kiki, gesturing.

"Many of the small cities are recovering. Even some of the larger ones, like Tucson. Phoenix has a long way to go. Much of the city burned. A lot of people died even before the plagues hit. Without water, casualties soared. But we're coming back."

"How long before the U.S. goes back to California?"

"We'll have to talk to Ron and the president about that. I don't know."

"Do we have to go back to LA?"

"Not for a while. We're on R & R."

Kiki looked at the kids splashing in the pool, then at the clean desert sky. She didn't want to go back.

Chapter Twenty-Five

It was Tuesday, rifle practice day. The firearms lessons had started three weeks after they arrived in Casa Grande. This was the fourth day of rifle practice. Thursdays were pistols. Tama loved Tuesdays. She leaned on the bench, nestled the buttstock of the AR-15 into her shoulder and inhaled. Most weekdays, they were alone at the gun-range south of Casa Grande. This twice-weekly routine was one the kids looked forward to. OJ was always exuberant about going to the range, Joel wasn't enthusiastic, doing it as a duty. Rosa treated it like a job. Shalene chose not to go. Tama always looked forward to it.

She let half of her breath out and sighted on the small black circle three hundred yards away. Though not Arizona-summer hot yet, heat waves caused the image to waver. She squeezed her whole hand as if squeezing a lemon. The rifle bucked against her in a light recoil.

"Nine ring, one-o'clock," said Kiki from the spotting scope beside her. This was Kiki's first chance to go to the range since her return to Casa Grande.

Tama focused again and fired.

"Nine ring, one-o'clock again. Nice group," praised Kiki. "Take a break."

Tama ejected the magazine and pulled the charging handle back, ejecting the cartridge. Locking the bolt open, she laid it on the bench.

Kiki observed her safety routine and nodded approval. Besides becoming an exceptional shot, Tama had learned proper safety procedures. Nick had taught her well.

"Let OJ take his turn." Tama moved to the seats behind the firing line, making room for OJ. Kiki watched him closely as he seated himself and went through the safety routine. Sitting back, he picked up the magazine, inspected it and fed in cartridges to replace those fired by Tama. He tapped the magazine, aligning the cartridges and inserted it in the gun. With the barrel pointed downrange, he pushed the slide release chambering a round. OJ glanced at Kiki. She nodded as he adjusted his earmuffs and sighted in on another target. He fired.

"Two ring, six-o'clock," Kiki said. He fired again. "White, three-o'clock." He fired again. "White, nine-o'clock." He fired again. "Miss." Kiki wanted to tell him to slow down and focus, but he'd heard it before. OJ knew what was needed, but held the excitement of a kid.

"Breathe, OJ," Joel said. "Calm down, concentrate, squeeze."

OJ started to say something. He glanced at Kiki. She nodded slightly. Joel was right. OJ turned back to the rifle, took a deep breath, let half out and grew still. The rifle bucked.

"X ring," said Kiki. "Joel's turn." She watched OJ go through the safety steps. He walked back to the bench with a smile.

Joel mechanically performed his safety steps. His shots were all in the black, but not grouped well. He would do okay, but he had not become one with the rifle, like Tama, like Kiki. "Rosa's turn," said Kiki.

Rosa went through the mechanics automatically. She learned quickly. Her shots were grouped nicely, but she treated the rifle as a tool, not an extension of herself.

"Let's pack it in," said Kiki. "We'll do pistol Thursday after school."

The quiet ride to the Sabino household gave Kiki time to think. They were training the kids for what? Was it necessary self-defense here in Casa Grande? Would she and Nick go back? What would happen to the kids if they left? Miriam and Stephen would take care of them.

Shalene and Miriam were preparing dinner when they got back. Tama and OJ helped while Joel and Rosa cleaned the AR-15. Kiki found Nick on the patio with a glass of wine. He poured for her as she sat.

"What's happening?" she asked.

"Ron called. We're to meet with him and David Kennedy at the Pinal Air Park tomorrow. Something's up." He watched Kiki as questions arose and held up a hand. "He didn't go into it."

"Nick, if we have to go back, what's going to happen to the kids, to Rosa and Monica?"

"Monica's settled in well, working at the restaurant. Her baby goes with her, so it works out, at least until she gets older. I'm not sure about Rosa. She's restless."

"Yeah, I noticed she goes through the motions, but there's something else she wants. Some of the kids display that, too. I keep thinking of them as kids, and they are, but what they've been through has hardened parts of them like adults. It's in their eyes. When Tama and OJ are shooting, the target is not what they see. The rifle is a part of them."

Nick nodded. "Yeah, I've noticed that too. It makes me worry about Joel. I identify with him because when I joined the Army, I wanted to be a medic, save people. Life since then gave me the hard edge to do what's needed." He sighed, feeling a twinge of regret. "I'm not sure it made me better."

"Dinner," called Miriam from the house.

As they went inside, Kiki wondered about herself. Why didn't she feel the regret about her targets, the people? Maybe she did, but she pushed it aside so easily. What she did was a job that had to be done. They were the enemy and there were always more.

Chapter Twenty-Six

"Boss, we may have something." Max walked into Sean's office. "When Katherine Russell was here with the Army, she roomed with a medic. We found records saying they were married. The guy's name was Nicholas Sabino."

Sean rose from behind his desk. He turned to the window, standing quietly. Max waited.

"I remember that name from my tour in the Sandbox. Can we find him?"

"I got guys on it now. We found her address in Marana, Arizona."

"Send someone to check it out. I want to hear back from them in a couple of days."

"Yeah, I thought that's what you'd want. I got guys gearing up now. Boss, the unit they were in when they came to LA was from Florence, Arizona.

Sabino has to be from Arizona. So far, our search on Sabino gives us Phoenix, Tucson, and Casa Grande. Oh yeah, and one in Yuma. Nicholas Sabino only came up in Casa Grande."

Sean turned to Max. "Our rescheduled summit is in two months. I want this bitch out of the picture by then. The new location is the community center in Ventura, Hijos' territory. It's not that we can't protect everyone, but it binds Hijos closer to us." Sean smiled slyly.

"Send guys to each of those places. I want you to go with them." He picked up the radio and called the Hijos. Sanchez answered. Without pleasantries, Sean said, "We have some leads on the assassins. I'm sending out search parties. Does Hijos want to be there?"

"Si'. I'll send four of my best guys. They'll be at your headquarters in a couple of hours."

Sean smiled at Max. "I like getting them involved. Less of our guys gone, and it brings us closer to Hijos. These Sabinos could be relations. Nicholas Sabino and Katherine Russell could be staying with them. You to go to Casa Grande. Check that out. I think that's where they are."

"You want I should kill them when we find them?"

"Max, it would make me much happier if you brought them back here alive. No, if you find them, lay low. Watch. If they get alerted that we've found them, they'll disappear. I want them, Max. I want them bad."

Max left the office to begin getting riders ready to leave in the morning. Two hours later with the Cs and the Hijos gathered around he explained the search. "We're looking for two people, Nicholas Sabino and Katherine Russell. I got no pix, but they're both early thirties. There's Sabinos in Phoenix, Tucson, Yuma, and Casa Grande. Check 'em out. The ones we're looking for will look military–fit, hair trimmed. They'll probably be together, so if you see someone like that, lay back and watch. Send word. Do not try to apprehend or capture. If you kill them, Sean will probably do the same to you. Understood?" Heads nodded. "We're leaving first light. Pack and get some rest. Questions?" There were none. "Oh, and try not to make any waves that get you noticed, that means leave your cuts behind."

Once, the trip from LA to Phoenix was less than six hours. Now, who knew? The freeways were clogged with wreckage and probably monitored, so they'd have to take other routes. They'd have to carry gas. A stop by bikers could alert someone. Most of the abandoned cars sat on the roads because they'd run out of gas.

"Shit!" Max exclaimed. He wasn't looking forward to hours on the bike.

There were three of them in each group, so if they found Sabino and Russell, someone would bring back the news. They had no radios that would work over the distance to LA, and cell phones would be monitored for sure.

Back as his room, he packed his gear. Civvy clothes for sure. He folded the Cs cut, the black leather vest with the Charon's Children emblem on top and put it on his bed. It wouldn't do to have that with him in case they did get stopped. Have to cover his tats, too.

Sean looked out his office window into the darkness of Los Angeles, only a few lights trying to push it back. His hatred for Katherine Russell rose within him like boiling lava. She had thwarted his plan to kill her in Afghanistan. She had wrecked the deal with Hijos de Hades for drugs, probably killed his brother, and she had delayed his summit to unite the gangs in Kalifornia.

In his mind's eye, he pictured her stretched between the flagpoles. He would take her skin off bit-by-bit. Then while she was still alive, he'd cut out her heart and eat it in front of her eyes as the life faded from them. His ears heard her screams.

His mind tingled at the images. Cold flowed in as he saw himself centered in her crosshairs. Fear clutched at his heart. If she found him first....

Chapter Twenty-Seven

Nick and Kiki lay together secure in darkness, their bedroom like a cocoon. The lovemaking had been slow and sensuous. The afterglow was a warm blanket. Kiki's mind prickled in a familiar and unwanted sensation. Oh no, not the Director. A glance at Nick and she knew he felt it, too. His eyes were open. The words formed in their minds.

"Good evening, Nicholas and Katherine. That lovemaking made the other namby-pamby part of me very happy. Too sweet for my taste. That is not why I am here. Your enemies will soon find you. Searchers seek you, and one party of them will come here. Their plan is to capture you alive. Sean wants to perform some really nasty business

on you. They fear you and foresee that you can destroy their plans. Sean Gallen gives me a particularly yummy mix of spicy hatred and sour fear. I will not like when it ends, but it must. I hope you will still be around. Be cautious."

They both lay stunned at this revelation. At last, Kiki spoke, "Nick, we have to leave again. If one of us has to go, it's going to be Sean."

"I know. We'll see what Ron and David say tomorrow, but we will have to go. I'll tell Brad about the danger coming. I hope he can protect the family."

"What about Rosa and Monica? The gangs don't know about the kids, but someone might know them."

"We'll deal with that. Time to get moving."

At the gate into the Pinal Airpark, the guard checked their IDs and waved them through. The morning air was crisp as a marine opened the door to the hangar. The small corporate jet was lit by overhead lights, the stairway extended. Ron Carson, Secretary of Interior was in the doorway and waved them forward. David Kennedy, Director of the CIA, was the only other person aboard. He stood as they entered.

"It's good to see you both again. Katherine, you look like you've recovered nicely."

"It was a close thing," said Nick. "The infection was aggressive and fast. We nearly lost her." He put his arm around her. Ron gestured to chairs surrounding a small table. "Coffee?" he asked. "I can make a fresh pot."

They shook their heads. David Kennedy cleared his throat. "My sources tell me you've done good things, disrupted Gallen's plans, at least for a while. It will take him weeks if not months to put together another summit."

"We don't want to wait for that," said Ron. "We want to be more aggressive, cause Gallen more problems and divert his attention away from this unity. He has made smart moves on the economic front, reviving business, getting his own economy going. The Imperial Valley is producing food for export. He has set up a banking system to support the farmers."

"Yeah, we heard a little about that," said Nick. "The Cs bring in slave labor. They make sweeps of the cities and pick up people to work the farms."

"Ugh," grunted Ron. "We thought that was just a rumor. Gallen's also got Silicon Valley operating. Hardware and software are among his most profitable products. Any resistance is squashed. He killed several corporate presidents to make his point. It worked."

"Gallen is moving to build California into a viable country," said David. "We want you to go back and disrupt those plans again. The best way would be for you to recruit locals to form a guerrilla force. You can pull people and resources away from his rebuilding efforts until we can bring in military forces."

Nick and Kiki looked at each other. "There are a couple of things you need to know," said Nick. "We believe Sean has sent a team to capture or kill us."

"How did they find you?" asked Ron.

"They have access to military records. Probably did a search on my name. Our unit came from Arizona, hence not such a big search."

"We can send in people to protect you," said Kennedy.

"There's more," said Kiki. "You know we came out with other people."

"Yeah, five kids and two women, as I recall," said Ron.

"Three of the kids and one woman know the territory and the people. They would be valuable assets in this plan of yours." Out of the corner of her eye, Kiki saw Nick frowning at her.

"You can't take them back," exclaimed Nick.

"Volunteer basis," said Kiki. "If they don't want to go, they stay."

"I can't condone using children and women in this fight," said Ron.

"Yet you have no problem sending me," said Kiki.

"You're a soldier," said Kennedy.

"And they will be, too. Unspeakable things were done to their families in front of them. I understand that, though not to the same extent. I saw my parents murdered only in my mind. They deserve the right, more than that, they need to be part of any move to make this right."

"But what about training?" asked Kennedy.

"Nick and I have been working with them. The new America requires that everybody have the ability to defend themselves. We've been teaching them." Kiki glanced at Nick. Fire seemed to be shooting from his eyes, directed at her. He was pissed, but she knew she was right.

"I'm having a problem with this," said Ron. "If the woman wants to go back, we'd welcome her help. The kids, I just can't do this."

"Ron, it's time you understood that there are few innocents in this war. And it is a war. You cannot undo what has happened to them, nor the consequences to them. It is my idea that we use them in recruiting. Others trust them and they are familiar with the territory. Those are assets we cannot afford to ignore. What you don't understand is that the gangs have almost wiped out the adult population. You want a guerrilla army? It won't be adults. We've been there and seen that."

Nick spoke up. "She's right. The only adults we saw were gang members or slaves. They were very thorough in removing any leadership or authority. As much as I hate to say it, using the local assets, kids, is the only way this can move forward. We can bring in a DI from Pendleton to work with them."

"Christ! This puts us on the same level as those who used children to spread smallpox," exclaimed Ron. "That was the beginning of this whole decline of civilization."

"Let's not make a decision now," said Kennedy, holding up a hand. "You and Katherine go back to Casa Grande. Give us a day to think this over. This is certainly something the president can never know about. It will be a decision made by those of us sitting here right now. Talk to your kids, too. See what they say."

Chapter Twenty-Eight

The ride back to Casa Grande began icily quiet, the silence pregnant. "Okay," said Kiki, "let's get this out. You think I was wrong about using the kids."

Nick's lips tightened. "Yeah, I did. K. It blindsided me at first. The suggestion pissed me off. It seems so wrong, but you're right. There is no choice if we're to put together a guerilla force. By definition, guerilla is native. Kids are the natives, but the idea of exposing them to the horrors of war–"

"Nick, the horrors they've already been exposed to are at least as bad. Watching your parents slaughtered."

"K, the difference is they will likely have to kill."

Look what that's done to me, thought Kiki.

"Is that what we want? Whatever the cause, it will change them," said Nick.

Look what's it's done to you. "In this new world," stated Kiki, "innocence is a luxury we can't afford."

Again, silence filled the car. Kiki watched the spiked mountain, Picacho Peak, as they passed. Her mind drifted back to her life on her parents' ranch with her family. If her daughter Lindy were alive, she would be younger than Tama. Would she send Lindy into this mess? No! In her mind, Lindy would always remain an innocent child. Kiki would always want her to be innocent. But that was an era when the world was sane.

***

Kiki looked at Joel, Tama, OJ and Rosa around the table on the Sabino patio. Monica was still at the restaurant with her daughter. Shalene was helping her. That was okay. She glanced toward the sparkling lights of Casa Grande below. Tears filled her eyes. She knew what the answer would be when she asked Rosa and the kids if they would return. It would mean some of them might die–or worse.

Kiki looked at the stars overhead, wiped her eyes and started. "Nick and I will be returning to Los Angeles to fight the Cs." Rosa and the kids looked at each other. "We have a mission to disrupt the plans of the Cs to organize into a government. Part of that mission is to recruit others in this fight. We could use help." Kiki left that hanging for a few minutes. Nick watched her.

OJ spoke immediately, "I'll go."

Kiki nodded. He still had innocence and enthusiasm born from a lack of understanding war, understanding what it meant to be a deadly aggressor. He lacked the compassion that age would bring. She held up her hand.

"I don't want answers from you now. Talk this over among yourselves. This is an important decision, one that will change your lives. We will be inside if you have questions, but this is for you to decide individually. Do not pressure each other. Going back will change you. It may kill you."

She and Nick rose and went into the house.

"We have to let them work this out, Nick. We'll talk to each one later before we accept their decision. The decision must be theirs."

"I understand. So what is the vision you have for them?"

"I'm not sure. My own priority had been Sean Gallen, the man who put a price on my head. It helps the cause of the president and the U. S., so okay."

"Is that what the kids are for, to help you get Sean?"

"No, Nick! I wouldn't do that."

"But you are. They're assets in your operation.

Kiki sat quietly, her mind in turmoil. She was using them, putting their lives on the line. Her mind prickled. She looked at Nick. He sensed it too and nodded at her.

"Bit of a quandary, Katherine? You need their help, but how will you feel when one dies in your service? Guilt is a bitter flavor, not one I enjoy."

"Nick, help me here," wailed Kiki.

"K, you know how I feel about involving the kids. Perhaps we could keep them safe, not use them on the front line. They would recruit and feed us info. No contact with the Cs."

"Nick, do you really believe you could keep them safe in Los Angeles? I would like you to take them. The fear in children is so spicy and clear. It is quite refreshing."

"You're disgusting," exclaimed Kiki.

"Really! You are the ones creating this, not me. You do not yet understand how special they are. I am going to enjoy them whatever you do."

Kiki tried to shut down her thoughts to drive this creature away. It fed on emotions, and she had learned when she controlled them, it would leave her alone.

"Nice control, Katherine. I do so enjoy conversing with you and Nick. Perhaps I should speak with others."

"Others would see you as the devil," exclaimed Kiki.

"But you and Nick do not."

"We do, and we don't. You have helped us. We see more because there are many aspects of you, good and love being among those. You could be lying about them. We have no way of knowing."

"I have no reason to lie. I/we are a species who exist in another plane from your physical world, who feed on human emotions. Yes, there are parts of me who like the flavors of love. This part of me enjoys the emotions of hatred and fear. And I like conversing with you."

Nick and Kiki sat mute, nothing to say. Still, the worry about how to handle the children niggled at Kiki's mind. They turned toward the sliding door to see OJ standing with his mouth agape.

"Who was that you were talking to? Where is he?" OJ glanced around the room.

"You heard the voice?" asked Kiki. OJ nodded. Oh God, thought Kiki. The Director has gone after the kids. "OJ, we don't know what that is. We call it the Director."

"It said it was a species, like a spirit or a ghost. It said it feeds off people. Is it evil?"

"In some ways it is. It causes people to do bad things. The people have a choice, but they do them under the influence of the Director."

"You said it helped you. Was that a bad thing?"

From the mouths of babes, thought Kiki. "No, Nick and I do good things, like fighting the Cs" *And some not good things like destroying men's minds.* The wails of those in the isolation chamber crying to their god filled her head.

"Not always good, eh, Katherine?"

OJ's eyes and mouth flew wide open.

"I do like the sharp spiky flavor of your fear, Oliver."

"It's OJ. I don't like Oliver."

"OJ, control your fear and hatred. It feeds on those," exclaimed Kiki. "Don't let it into your mind."

"Hmmmm. Let us see how good you are at controlling your emotions."

Kiki watched OJ's face contort in horror. Whatever the vision was, she had to get OJ away from it. "OJ," she cried, "look at me." She grabbed him by the shoulders and shook him. His eyes focused on her. "It can't hurt you. It can only put visions into your mind."

"I saw the murder of my family."

"It did the same to me, OJ. I know what it is doing. I know what you're feeling. Let it go. Let it go."

His face scrunched up and tears flowed down his cheeks. She hugged him to her as he shook with great sobs. "Leave us, Director," she wailed.

"There is that sour flavor of guilt within you, Katherine. Do you think you are the reason I talked to Oliver? You do not influence me, I do that to you."

Kiki fought for control, finally joining OJ with her sobs.

Chapter Twenty-Nine

Max stared at the dilapidated ranch house. Their trip from California to Marana had taken two days as they traveled the back roads, avoiding roadblocks and inspections. His butt hurt. He looked at the collapsed porch, the roof to the house missing in places. No unbroken windows remained and the door hung on one hinge. No one had lived there for years. If this was Katherine Russell's house, she was staying away. Carefully, he entered, mindful of the creaky floor. Dust and trash lay thickly. It smelled of dung.

He went back into the yard, Bing, his other C following. Facing the Hijo, Roberto, Max explained. "Bing's going back to LA." He turned to Bing. "Tell Sean this was a dead end. Nobody's been here in a long time, probably since Russell's family was killed. Roberto and I are going to Casa Grande to scope that out."

He took a last look at the ranch house ruin. *Where have you been since you shot up our summit meeting, Katherine? If not your place, then your husband's?*

"Sean will probably send you back here. Get us on the radio when you're near Casa Grande. Stay off the grid."

Roberto spoke up. "Cross the border and drive Comino Dos in Mexico. The contacts in Sasabee will get him back across the border at Mexicali. He needs to avoid any surveillance. Here, I will show you on the map."

Max nodded. Traveling in Mexico made sense. While they talked, he took a leak at a nearby mesquite. *Pretty country here. Must have been a good ranch when it was running. A nice place to grow up.*

Max remembered the time when Andros disappeared. When the boss of Niños de Noche disappeared from Albuquerque, Andros sent Max to get the club back on track. Niños had the heroin connection out of Mexico. It was white powder smack that was coming across the border, not

Mexican brown. To pay for it, both Charon's Children and Niños were doing contract killings. First their Arab contact disappeared, then Andros.

Was this sniper, Katherine Russell, really behind this? Or was Sean fixated, the pressure getting to him? Could he really pull off the unification of California and form a new country? If anyone could, it was Sean. He zipped up and walked back.

"Bing, you got what you need?" He nodded. "See you in a few days. Saddle up."

They took the back roads, staying away from Tucson. Heading west, Bing split to the south, and he and Roberto went north on the Reservation roads. Two hours later, they came to Casa Grande from the south.

"Where you guys going?" asked the deputy at the checkpoint. A rifle barrel was visible in the guard shack behind him,

"We're heading east but gotta stop in Phoenix. Been riding since Ajo. Need a break."

"Yeah, welcome to Casa Grande. Down this street and to the right toward I-10 are several eating places. Pretty good food. Don't stay too long."

The barricade rose and they motored through. Behind them, the deputy put the radio to his mouth.

"Brad, you there? Over."

"Go ahead. Over," came the reply.

"Just had a couple of bikers come in through the reservation road. Said they were going to get something to eat and go on to Phoenix. Over."

"They showing any gang sign? Over."

"Nope, but they were pretty well covered, so I couldn't see any ink. Might want to take a look. Over."

"I might take a drive up café row and check them out. Thanks. Over."

There were several quick food places and a couple of restaurants. One caught Max's eye, Cocina de Sabino. There had to be a tie to Nicholas Sabino. He nodded to Roberto.

The restaurant was better than quick food. It was also nearly empty. They chose a table near the window so they could see the street, but back far enough to not be visible from it. A waitress came in from the kitchen, but turned around and went back through the door. Curious, thought Max.

Monica leaned against the wall of the kitchen shaking. "What's wrong?" asked Stephen.

"I recognize one of those men. He is one of the Hijos de Hades gang. He did things to my family." She shuddered.

"I'll go out. You stay in here. Don't let them see you." Monica nodded, biting her lip to keep from screaming.

Stephen took the menus from Monica's hand as he went into the dining room. One of the guys was big and shaggy, his greasy hair tied into a ponytail. The other was slight, smallish build, darker complexion hinting at Hispanic heritage.

"Afternoon, guys," said Stephen, laying the menus on the table. "Welcome to Cocina de Sabino. What can I get you to drink?"

"Couple of waters and a couple of Buds," said Max.

"No Bud, but we have a local beer."

"Yeah, that'll do," said Max

"You got it," said Stephen.

Back in the kitchen, he called Sheriff Brad Tierman. "Brad, we have a couple of guys in the restaurant. Monica recognized one as a gangbanger from LA."

"Yeah, I got a call when they came into town. I'll be there in ten. Let me in the back door."

"Monica, the sheriff's coming. Get yourself a glass of water and sit for a few minutes." She nodded and allowed Stephen to guide her to a chair.

Stephen opened the door to Brad's soft tap. "They're at the table back from the window."

Brad peered through the window in the swinging door. "Yeah, okay. Think I'll go have a talk with them." He pushed through the door and walked to their table. "Afternoon, guys." The big guy looked up. His eyes hardened.

"Sheriff." No other expression on his face. Brad looked at the Hispanic. He stared down at the table. "What can we do for you?" asked the big guy.

"I understand you guys came from Ajo. What's it like over there? We don't get much news." Brad pulled out a chair and sat at the table. "I'm Sheriff Tierman." He held out his hand.

The big guy took it. "Max. This is Roberto. We're coming up from Mexico. Been there about six months. When all the trouble started we got across the border at Mexicali as fast as we could. Money ran out. We're heading north and east through Phoenix."

Brad nodded. It was a good story, explained the California plates on the bikes and the trip through Ajo. "Anything happening in Ajo?"

"Nah. Immigration and Customs are about dead. Guess they pulled most of the people out. Only Mexicans manning the posts. Think we'd have more trouble going back."

Another good story. It matched what Brad already knew. "Heard anything about California? We don't know what's going on there."

"Nothing since we left. Not much news going south. Gangs moved in, some cartels too. Don't wanna go back there."

"Have a good trip." Brad rose.

"Say, when I was in Afghanistan, a medic saved my buddy's life. His name was Sabino. He was from Arizona. Any chance this name," he looked around the restaurant, "is related?"

Brad turned back. "Nick Sabino lived here. He went to Afghanistan as a medic, but he hasn't been back here in years. Don't know where he is now, if he's still alive. One report was that he'd been killed in a helicopter crash, but it wasn't confirmed. His brother owns this place. If you hear anything, he'd like to know about Nick. His dad died earlier this year and we were hoping Nick would come back, but he didn't."

"Thanks. See you, Sheriff. I'll get word back if I find out anything." Max raised a hand, signaling the conversation was over.

Brad shrugged, turned and walked away. These guys would bear watching. I need to call Nick.

Chapter Thirty

Warm wind blew across the Sabino patio and the three children sitting around the table. "Joel, I got to go back," said Tama, with a grim face. "I can't let the Cs go free. They killed my family, made me watch. I'll fight them and what they've done. I hate them."

"Me too," exclaimed OJ. "I wanna kill them all." He paused, feeling the hatred rising in him, something he hadn't been aware of before. *Was the Director feeding on him now?* He shuddered at the memory of what the Director had done.

"Tama, OJ, I hate 'em, too," said Joel. "They murdered my family, stole my friends. I want things to be like before. That's probably not going to happen, no matter what. I'm not sure what I can do against them."

"You can fight them, kill them," snarled OJ. His voice was so out of place for a twelve-year-old.

"I...I don't know. I couldn't shoot that man."

"Joel, he was a C," exclaimed Tama.

"He was a man, a person."

"He was an evil man. Look what he was doing to Rosa and Monique. They were slaves. He was raping them," cried Tama.

Joel stood, his head down, shoulders slumped.

"Joel, I agree we'll never have what we had before, but we have to do something. If not us, who? The United States will come back." She looked at OJ. He was quiet. "What do you think?"

His gaze moved from Tama to Joel. "The Cs scare me. They scare me a lot. But I can fight them. You can too, Joel."

All three heads turned as they heard the ringing of the phone inside.

"Hello," answered Nick.

"Hey Nick, it's Brad. There's a couple of bikers in *Cocina de Sabino*. Monica recognized one of them from the Hijos gang. They're being here is no coincidence. One asked about you, claiming he knew you in Afghanistan. Said he wanted to catch up. I gave them a story about you not being back here for years, but they'll still check around. Too many people are aware you're in town. It won't hold water."

"Yeah, and once they realize you lied, they'll know we're here. Let me talk this over with Kiki. I'll get word to you quick."

He turned to Kiki. "They found us."

The deer in the headlights look crossed her face. "What'll we do?"

Nick related his conversation with Brad.

Her expression hardened. "We take 'em. We need to find out what they know."

"I'll call Ron. We'll get the chamber here to question them. We need answers fast."

"Do we involve Brad in this?" Kiki asked. "We can't take them alone, and we need to hold them until the chamber arrives."

The more people who know about this, the riskier for them. Nick punched a number into his phone. "Brad, do you have pictures of these guys?"

"Of course."

"Send them. We may have eyewitnesses pegging them with murder."

Kiki looked a question at Nick.

His phone dinged that a message had arrived. He opened the attached photo. "Recognize these guys?" he asked Kiki.

She looked. "The big guy was at the meeting you and I disrupted. Don't recognize the other one."

"Hey, guys what you looking at?" asked Tama.

Before Nick could object, Kiki held out the phone. "Recognize either of these guys?"

Tama looked and gasped in horror. Her face paled. "That big guy," she stuttered, "is the one who killed my family. Where did you get this?"

Nick hit redial. "Brad, our eyewitnesses say that at least one committed murder. Kiki and I will be down in ten minutes. You got tasers?"

"Yeah."

"Kiki, let's go. Kids, we'll be back in a little while. Hang here." As they left the house, Nick called Ron Carson. "Ron, where's the isolation chamber?"

"Don't muck around with pleasantries, do you? Yeah, Nick thanks for asking. I'm doing fine. The chamber is in storage at the Naval Air Station in San Diego. Why?"

"The Cs found us. There's a couple of guys here in Casa Grande. One's with the Cs, the other is with Hijos. We have witnesses they committed murder. We need to question them."

"It'll be on a plane to Pinal Air Park today. I'll make arrangements for you. Are you and Kiki all right?"

"Yeah, for now. Been talking to the kids."

Ron grunted. "How'd that go? Wait, we'll talk about that later. See you there."

The thought of interrogating with the isolation chamber sent a shiver through Nick. Worming his way into another person's mind and dragging out his most closely held secrets comes with consequences, mostly for the victim. It was violence intimate.

Chapter Thirty-One

Nick and Kiki stepped around the sheriff's cruiser and tapped on the *Cocino de Sabino* service door. Brad opened, it stepping aside to let them in. "Stephen's taking their order now. They're the only ones in the dining room." He reached for his radio. "I'll call for backup."

"Don't," said Nick. "Nobody else can know about this. You have to forget it, too. Can you do that?"

"Why? We'll arrest them and hold them for trial."

"Brad, if anybody but us knows about these guys, it will lead to Kiki and me. Really bad guys will show up, people will get hurt or worse."

"What are you going to do with them? You gonna kill them? I can't allow that." He scowled at Nick and Kiki.

Nick glanced at Kiki. "Brad, we won't kill them. I promise." They both were thinking the same thing. *It's worse than that.* They palmed the tasers and left through the rear door, heading around to the front entrance.

***

Max watched the couple enter. The woman was small, dark hair, dark complexion. The guy was tall, slender. They had their arms around each other. As they moved toward a near table, Max noticed something familiar about his face. It was a little like the waiter's face, same nose, same eyes. Could it be…? Max rose, turned at the sound of the kitchen door opening. He saw the sheriff, turned toward the couple. His eyes widened as the dart struck. His ears heard the thump as Roberto's body hit the floor, or was it his own?

Brad looked at the two bodies. "Now what?" he asked.

Nick and Kiki handed the spent tasers to him. "Go ahead and return to your office. With Stephen's help, we'll move these two out of town. You know too much already, but it couldn't be helped. Thanks, Brad."

The sheriff returned to the kitchen as Stephen came through the door into the dining room. He gaped at the still forms lying on the floor. Nick knelt and injected each. "That will keep them out for several hours." He and Kiki striped their shirts off and rolled them onto their stomachs, putting plastic ties on their hands, securing their ankles. Gags went into their mouths. "Stephen, bring your truck to the service door. How long as it been since you rode a bike?"

Stephen's attention snapped back to Nick. "A couple of years, but I can still manage."

"We'll load these two into your truck. Kiki will drive it. Two bikers need to be seen leaving the city, so we'll follow her through the gate and north on I-10. She'll take the first exit past Casa Grande and find a deserted spot. The bikes go in the back and we'll go to the house to get our overnight gear and SUV. We'll drive the truck and Kiki will follow us to Pinal Air Park. After we unload our cargo, you return. Business as usual from there." The puzzled look on Stephen's face told him this was moving fast. "You got it? Any questions?"

"Naw, okay. Let me call Barb so she can take over here." Stephen walked back to the kitchen.

"K, we need to tell the kids we'll be gone for two days. That should be enough time to get the info."

"The truck's in the alley," said Stephen as he returned.

Lifting Roberto and moving him to the truck was easy. Max was another matter. With Kiki picking up his feet, Stephen and Nick each took an arm. They half-dragged and half-carried him up the ramp. In the kitchen, Nick and Stephen donned the bikers' shirts and helmets,

"Why is the delivery truck in the alley?" Stephen's wife, Barb asked as she came into the kitchen. Her eyebrows rose as she saw Stephen and Nick in the biker garb.

"Don't ask," said Stephen. "We have something to do and best if you know nothing for now. I'll fill you in later. Have Monica come out of the office and straighten up the dining room. Watch the place. I'll be back in a couple of hours. It's okay, Hon."

Barb stepped aside as Kiki squeezed past her and out the door to the truck. Nick and Stephen went out the front. The rumble of the bikes was the only sound on the street. As Nick turned for a last check, Barb was peering through the front window.

"She going to be all right?" he asked.

"Yeah. I'm sure Monica will fill her in on some of it."

They fell in behind the delivery truck and headed toward I-10. The guard at the checkpoint waved the familiar truck through, his attention fixed on the two bikers following. As they passed through, he radioed the sheriff. "The bikers are leaving town."

"Roger," said Brad. "Thanks. Nick would fill him in on what he need to know later."

Nick and Stephen followed the truck as it took the Sacaton exit and drove west toward the Gila River. Kiki stopped at a deserted spot. Before she could get out of the cab, Nick raised the roll-up door and slid the ramp out. He and Stephen drove the bikes inside and secured them. In less than five minutes, they were heading back to the interstate and Casa Grande.

At the Sabino household, Kiki and Nick grabbed some overnight things. The interrogations might take a few days. The kids sitting in the den sprang up as Nick and Kiki entered.

Kiki faced them. "We need to talk." She sat. Nick and Stephen stood to one side. "I'm sure

Tama told you about the picture I showed her." They nodded. "There were two bikers in town." She held up her phone with the picture of the Hispanic. "Rosa, do you recognize this man?"

She looked and sucked in her breath. "He is with the Hijos. He killed Monica's husband."

"We have them. They can't hurt you. We will be gone for a few days. You are safe, but it is important that you say nothing about them, not even to Nick's mom. Stephen's helping us, and Barbara knows some, but it is best if you don't speak about these guys to anybody except yourselves. Can you do that?" They nodded.

"Are you gonna kill them?" asked OJ. The kids and Rosa awaited her answer.

"We need to ask them some questions."

"And then you're going to kill them?" asked Joel.

"We're not going to kill them," said Kiki, "but they won't ever harm anybody again. What they tell us may influence our return to LA. We'll talk about it when we get back." Kiki walked over and gave each a hug. OJ hung on for a few seconds. She unwrapped his arms. "See you in a few days. Tell

Mrs. Sabino we had to go out of town but we didn't tell you anything else."

Stephen drove the truck with Nick as a passenger while Kiki followed in their SUV. Nick looked at Stephen. "You do understand why these guys have to evaporate without a trace, right?"

"I do, but I'm still coming to grips with it. It's one thing to hear about bad guys, about you and Kiki taking care of them. It's quite another to be hit with the reality of it, to lay hands on two guys who will disappear. You told Brad and the kids you wouldn't kill them. Is that the truth?"

"Yeah. Nobody is going to kill them. They're going to a lockup forever."

Stephen's voice rose. "No trial or anything?"

"If they confess, they'll be gone. We won't need a trial."

"What if they don't confess?"

"Oh, they will," said Nick, his voice low.

"You're going to torture them, aren't you?"

"We will not lay a hand on them. They will freely admit what they've done."

Bewilderment covered Stephan's face. "How…?"

Nick held up a hand halting Stephen's inquiry. "That's all I can tell you. Best if you don't ask more."

Stephen seemed focused on the road, but Nick knew his mind was turning over what had happened and what would happen. The trip continued in silence until Stephen asked, "When will you be back?"

"Couple of days at least. Depends on what we find out."

Chapter Thirty-Two

At the Pinal Air Park gate entry, Nick gave his name, and the guard waved them through, directing them toward a large hangar. Another soldier with an M-4 slung on his shoulder pulled open the sliding door. It was dark inside with the windows painted over. From out of the gloom, Ron Carson appeared at the driver's side window. No one else was in the cavernous building.

"Stephen, good to see you again." Ron shook his hand. "The C-130 will be here within the hour."

"We need to unload the truck so Stephen can get back to Casa Grande before he's missed," said Nick. "Where do we put the cargo?"

"What shape are they in?"

"Both are out for another couple of hours. Other than that, they're unharmed."

"Let's take them back to the locker room." Ron pointed to a door at the side of the hangar.

"Right. Better get a tarp to cover the bikes in case someone comes in," said Nick.

"No one's coming in. I have guards at the exits."

Nick and Stephen rolled the bikes down the ramp and pushed them to one side while Ron and Kiki dragged the smaller Hispanic into the locker room. It took the four of them to drag the big guy in.

Nick put his hand on Stephen's shoulder. "Best if you go. Tell your wife only what you have to. The same with Brad." Nick gave him a hug.

As he stepped into the cab of the truck, Kiki kissed him on the cheek. "Take care. Here's Ron's number." She handed him a slip of paper. "Memorize it. If anything happens, call. We'll get you help."

"Tell Brad I'll keep my promise. We'll be fine. Back as soon as we can, not more than a couple of days." Nick slapped him on the back.

Ron pulled open the door so Stephen could drive through. He called the front gate to give him passage. Turning to Nick he asked, "How many people know about this?"

"Three plus the kids and Rosa and Monica. They won't say anything. Let's go learn about our guests. They returned to the locker room and the prostrate figures. Nick put on latex gloves from his bag and began checking them. He pulled out their IDs.

Nick tapped the Hispanic with his toe. "This one is Roberto Gallardo Cardenas. His driver's license is Mexican." He tucked the ID into his pocket. "This one is Maxwell Bolger, Salt Lake City address." He counted the cash in Max's wallet. "He's loaded. More than a thousand bucks."

"Traveling money," commented Kiki. "When I last saw this man, I could have had him in my sights but shot a bigger guy instead."

"No regrets," admonished Nick. "If it wasn't him lying here, it would be someone else." Kiki searched Roberto while Nick checked Max's pockets as the striped him. "Like his old boss, Andros, I see nothing religious. Don't know if he's an atheist or not."

"Roberto has religious tats along with the Hijos ink," pointed out Kiki. "Looks like he was raised

Catholic but probably not practicing lately." She stared at the long scars across his back. "This boy's been abused, but not in a while."

As they arranged the two nude figures on the concrete, the roar of turboprop engines shook the building. The doors opened, and the giant transport taxied in. With the doors closing behind it, the engines wound down. The silence was abrupt.

The whine of a loading ramp lowering was followed by a clang as it settled on the concrete. Nick, Kiki and Ron entered the cavernous hold. Lights came on, spotlighting a room-sized wooden box. As Nick approached the box, the cockpit door opened. "Stay inside," ordered Ron. The door closed.

Nick stepped into the box, flipped a switch and scanned the inside. A black coffin-like box was against one side. The surface absorbed the light, giving no reflection. It sat atop a foam cushion. He pulled out his tablet, walked around taking inventory, noting things.

"Need help?" asked Kiki, peering through the doorway. Her eyes fixed on the black box momentarily.

"I'll check this out. You and Ron move Roberto on board. Use one of the gurneys against the wall. Yell when you want help with Max and the bikes. I have to make up a list of things we need."

As Kiki left, Nick opened the lid of the isolation chamber. It had been flushed and cleaned. The connectors allowing them to monitor life functions showed signs of corrosion, so Nick added replacements to the list. The medications were out of date, more to put on the list. He added water to the chamber and started the heater and circulating pump. The water moved without a sound and the thermometer showed the temperature stabilizing at ninety-eight point six. Monitor screens on the wall of the chamber lit. The electronics were working.

He stepped back and looked at the chamber. He shook his head, remembering the others he had questioned. It had all been necessary, but was it right?

Kiki's call from the cargo hold startled him. "Need your help with Max, Nick. You all right?"

"Yeah, coming."

Both gurneys were secured to the deck, the figures draped with sheets. The bikes were driven aboard and locked down, then hidden beneath covers. The hangar showed no signs of them. Ron looked at the list Nick had made. "I'll send this to University Medical Center." He glanced at Nick and Kiki. "We have a chopper to take you to pick up what you need. I'm going to run these two guys through the information system to see what I can find."

Nick nodded. Some of the drugs he needed were exotic and they might have to substitute. "K, best if you stay here. You're more recognizable than me, and we don't know who's out looking or where they may be. And somebody has to stay with these two guys."

Her mouth opened to object, then closed. "How long will they be out?" she asked pointing.

He held up two syringes. "If either wakes." How ironic that they were draped like bodies, Nick thought. He looked around the hold. Nothing showed to indicate their cargo. "Let's give the pilots a break."

Ron escorted the two men from the plane. "We'll call when we need you. Stay on base." They nodded. A typical black operation.

Chapter Thirty-Three

Rosa sighed, looking at the kids, then out the sliding glass door to the Sabino patio. "My sisters are still in Los Angles. Los Hijos killed my husband, my mother, my father." She shuddered. "They made me a slave. I must make them answer for these crimes."

Tama spoke next, "Me, too. My world came apart because these animals stole their vaccine."

Rosa watched her. Compassion for her was selective. Deep for Joel, OJ and Shalene. It was nonexistent for her enemies. She was growing like Kiki.

Joel's head was down. "I want to go back," he whispered, "but I don't know if I can... do what's needed. I couldn't shoot that man at the camp. I wanted to, but my finger froze."

"I could do it," said OJ. "I could kill them."

Rosa looked at the intensity on his face. *So young, so much hatred.* She felt for Joel. Her sister Monica was like him, wanting only to help people. She glanced at the faces. They were not much younger than she was, in years, but perhaps older in experience. They had lived in the ruins of Los Angeles.

"Joel," said Tama gently, "Kiki told me Nick went into the army as a medic. He carried a medical bag, not a weapon."

"I know," said Joel. "Nick told me. But he changed."

"What happened?"

"He had to protect someone he loved. That was Kiki."

"We'll need another medic," said Joel. "Could I be trained?"

"We'll need trainers for all of us," said Tama. "Nick can work with you."

They were encouraging Joel, Rosa realized. Tama wanted them to stay together. Rosa realized she wanted to be with them. They, along with her sister and niece, were all the family she had.

"How long before we can go back?" asked OJ.

"Nick mentioned bringing in a drill instructor," said Joel. "He and Kiki taught us the basics of shooting and weapons, but that's not enough."

"There is much to learn if we are to fight these bastardos," said Rosa. "My brother was in the army. They had basic training for eight weeks before moving on to specialist training. He was in the infantry. Got killed in Afghanistan."

"Eight weeks!" exclaimed OJ. He frowned.

"With that Hijo and that C showing up, the time might change," said Rosa.

"Do you think they killed them?" asked OJ. "I hope so." Rosa watched his expression change from hatred to fear. He shuddered. *What was going on inside him? Something powerful.*

"Nick and Kiki have to find out what they know, so they're not dead yet," said Tama, a thin smile on her lips.

Rosa shivered at the thought of how Nick and Kiki would get the answers they sought. She had watched friends being tortured just because they were alive, not because they had important information. "Nick said our mission is to help recruit more fighters," said Rosa, changing the subject. "I can get more of the people who are slaves to the Hijos, but we must free them. Then we have to train them. A big job."

Tama looked at Joel. "We know groups, mostly kids. They'll need training, too."

He nodded agreement.

"So we recruit more fighters!" exclaimed OJ. "What for? I mean what are we going to do? I want to kill Cs." Again, his expression changed from hatred to fear. His mouth snapped shut.

"I think," started Rosa, "we are going to be trained as trainers."

"I don't want to be a trainer," interrupted Tama.

"Me either," exclaimed OJ. "I want to fight."

This time, OJ's expression was restrained as if he was holding back. She would have to find out more about the inside of OJ's head. "I want the world to be what it was before," said Rosa. "I'll do whatever I'm told to get that back. If I get to take revenge on the way that's okay." She watched the heads nodding around her. "I also fight for my sister."

Chapter Thirty-Four

Bing rode into the parking lot at the LA arena. The two heads on the flagpoles were skulls now, the flesh picked off by the crows. The smell of death still hung in the air, but not a reek. It had been a long ride, and he needed a beer before facing Sean. He'd seen Sean go off before when receiving bad news. Lucky for him, his news wasn't bad, but not altogether good. Beer in hand, he knocked on Sean's office door.

"Come." Sean folded his hands on his desk and looked him up and down. "So, anything?"

Bing shuffled his feet, then stood straight. "The ranch was a bust. No one there for a long time. Max sent me back with the report. He and Roberto went on to Casa Grande to check that out."

Sean frowned. "Yeah, Yuma and Tucson were busts, too. How was the trip back?"

"I took a route through Mexico. Glad I had the protection of the Hijos. There were a few roadblocks. Nothing official, Hijos outlaws. It wasn't until Mexicali that I ran into the Federales. They were looking to keep Americans from entering, so showed no concern if one crazy gringo wanted to go north. No U. S. Customs or Immigration at the border. It was weird to see it all deserted."

"How about the roads in the U. S.?"

"I stayed on the back roads, so not much to see until I neared the California border. The back road over the mountains gave me a view of the interstate highway. Lots of troops and stuff there."

"Yeah, that's what the other guys said. The reports I get say things are going good in the agro areas. How'd it look to you?"

"Lots of green, lots of people in the fields. Trucks loaded, ready to haul produce."

Sean had a rare smile on his face. "We're getting good cooperation from the farmers. They're getting free labor and no water or pesticides restrictions. Production is up."

"Max is going on to Phoenix if Casa Grande falls through. He wanted me to catch up with him, bring any news."

"We're still on track for a new summit in ten days. Hijos de Hades is going to host it in Ventura. That's why it's critical this Russell bitch is out of the picture. It would help our image if we had her stretched out screaming. It would make me very happy, too."

"I understand, Boss."

"No, you don't. Get yourself something to eat. Get some rest. Get back to Max day after tomorrow. We gotta keep this search hot."

"Right, Boss."

"Talk to me before you leave."

Bing looked at the clear blue sky as he left the arena. Los Angeles hadn't had many of those before the war. Funny how the lack of people cleared the sky. Motoring to his house, he marveled at how quiet the streets were. Once they got the wrecks and trash cleaned up, this could be a nice place. A couple of raids to pick up some people, and they'd have the labor needed. Maybe he'd mention that to Sean after he got back from Arizona.

He paused before entering the posh house, now his. *Wonder how Max is doing? Did he catch up with Russell and Sabino? Sure wouldn't want to be in their shoes if he did.*

Chapter Thirty-Five

The University Medical Center loomed below as the thirty-minute helicopter flight to Tucson ended on the helipad. Ron's message with Nick's list resulted in an orderly wheeling a cart toward the idling chopper.

"That list had some exotic stuff on it," he yelled as Nick helped him load the boxes. "We had to raid the experimental labs to get everything. What's it for?"

"Experiments," said Nick, "top secret experiments." The orderly's mouth clamped shut.

The engine roared and Nick watched the pad grow smaller. From the air, nothing seemed odd about the city, unless you noted the lack of people and cars. The loss of power from the damaged electrical grid during the attacks caused the loss of vital water pumping. Many of the elderly and ill had died. Weather related deaths were nothing like the northeast portions of the country.

Nick closed his eyes. Tucson had not been so lucky with the smallpox plague. The isolation policies had kept it from the city for a while. Medical facilities soon became overwhelmed. Almost one-third of Tucson's population perished.

Below he saw the city limits, manned by roving patrols, give way to desert and the patchwork of green fields of crops. Nick strained, trying to find Kiki's ranch, but he couldn't pick it out.

Thoughts of the tasks ahead rose in his mind. Using the isolation chamber for interrogations had been extremely successful. Nick extracted information in hours that would have taken days or weeks, or maybe never using conventional methods. The victims suffered no physical harm, no pain.

The key to opening them up was Nick's expertise. He could find the pathway into their minds that made them believe they were dead. Each person was different, harboring unique beliefs about death and what followed. Nick was the master at finding and exploiting that belief. It was good for Nick, bad for the person in the chamber.

All of his previous sessions had resulted in the mental destruction of those leaving the chamber. These were bad people, having committed the most heinous crimes, but to destroy someone's mind ate at Nick. He had never wanted to do it again, but here he was.

The helicopter touched down. Reluctantly, Nick began transferring the supplies toward the hangar with Kiki's help. "More to carry?" she asked. Nick nodded as he stowed the boxes in the maw of the giant plane. She went back to fetch the remaining supplies. Nick looked at the two figures shrouded on the gurneys.

As Kiki returned with the last packages, Ron came back from the cockpit. "I couldn't get much info on Roberto. The Mexicans are working on him. I got a lot on Max Bolger." He glanced at his tablet.

"Max ran with the Charon's Children in Salt Lake City as Andros Gallen's number two man. He went to Albuquerque to straighten out Hijos de Hades when their president disappeared. Charon's Children and Hijos de Hades had a business relationship–drugs for murder." He glanced at Nick and Kiki then back at his tablet.

Nick and Kiki's eyes locked. Pieces of the puzzle were falling into place.

Ron continued. "When Andros Gallen disappeared, Max returned to Salt Lake City to take over the chapter. Things stayed quiet for a while, but business wasn't good. The flow of drugs from Mexico became spotty. Gun smuggling hadn't worked out and the cops seemed to know what was going on. The club was broke." Ron smiled at this. He continued, "Andros' brother Sean came back from Afghanistan and took over from Max."

Ron looked up from the pad at Kiki. "The story gets interesting here. We think his Arab partners pressured him to set you up for an ambush. You were really hurting them." He smiled again. "The ambush failed to kill you, but you left Afghanistan after the death of your family. You were out of the picture, though not as satisfying to the Arabs as they wanted."

"Your family's murders were the first in the terrorist campaign against the dependents of serving soldiers in Afghanistan. Drugs from the Arabs paid for the murders specified by the terrorists."

Nick and Kiki knew this part of the story well.

"The murder-for-hire operation fell apart thanks to you two. Sean was also trying to set up a smuggling business to move confiscated weapons to his brother's club. Evidence against him started piling up, though nothing strong enough to bring charges, but Sean was booted from the military. He returned to Salt Lake City, taking over from Max." They all glanced at the shrouded figure on the gurney.

"You've got most of the story right," said Nick, his gaze moving to Kiki. She was like stone. The memories of her family's murder and the subsequent killings had pulled her mind away from here. He turned toward the shrouded gurneys. "We'll take Max first."

Chapter Thirty-Six

Nick checked both men. They were still unconscious, heartbeats slow but strong, breathing regular. He tightened the restraints on Roberto and wheeled Max into the compartment.

Ron and Kiki carried in the last of the supplies. "Let's get him stripped and into the chamber," said Nick. Lifting Max took all three of them. They put the naked form on a scale. Nick entered his weight into his laptop. "Nice ink," he noted, inspecting the tattoos, mostly gang tats, nothing religious.

Nick turned toward the black box. He reached out to open the casket-like hinged lid and paused. He didn't want to do this, but they needed the information these guys had. With the lid open, the box gaped like a maw. They struggled to lay Max inside. Nick secured him with soft restraints, attached the monitor pads for pulse rate, respiration, body temperature, and blood pressure. He inserted the IVs. Nick attached the bone microphone and the brain function sensors to his head. He stepped back to see if he'd forgotten anything.

"The brine is mixed and heated," said Kiki, pointing at the large tank to one side. Nick opened a valve and the solution of Epsom salt and warm water flowed into the chamber. When Max floated freely, his face above the solution, Nick closed the valve and started the circulating pump. He checked his laptop to see that all the sensors were working.

The solution flowed around the inert form soundlessly. Nick took a last look at Max. *Goodbye, whoever you were.* He closed the lid, removing Max from this world.

Nick sat in a chair with his laptop with Kiki seated beside him. The monitor showed the figure in the chamber, his vitals in a panel to one side. Max appeared to be sleeping. "Ron you know the drill, no noise while the microphone is open. Write down any questions you want answered. We'll be recording everything if you choose to leave."

"I'll stay for a little while. I do have other things to do."

Nick nodded. "Okay, first I add the curanine to paralyze him." He watched the monitors as he started a drip. "Too much curanine and we'll paralyze his breathing. He'll suffocate. Too little and he'll thrash about in the chamber. It's a delicate balance that will change as things are added and as the questioning proceeds." Nick wanted to explain everything as clearly as possible, recording it so someone else could learn and do this instead of him. Yet, if he remained the only one, the use of this interrogation technique wouldn't become common. There was a level of immorality to it.

"Now we'll add some adrenaline to start waking him up." Nick watched Max's heart rate and breathing increase. "We'll scramble his thinking with a little hallucigen, LSD, and some amphetamine as he wakes." Through the infrared camera he watched Max's eyes open and begin blinking rapidly trying to see in the total darkness. Max's brain activity spiked.

"Where am I?" cried Max.

Nick left him in silence. Monitors showed increasing heart rate and breathing.

"Where am I? What's happened to me?" Max's voice rose. Within the chamber, sound cancelling technology kept him from hearing his own voice. He was totally isolated from his own senses, a mind floating in darkness.

Spikes in breathing and heart rate showed on the monitor. Max began to panic.

"Calm down, asshole," said Nick into the microphone.

"Who's that? Why can't I see? Why can't I move?"

Max's heart raced, his breath in shallow gasps. *"Quit fighting, you dickhead. It won't do any good. Took me a while to learn that."*

"You sound like Andros."

"That's because I am Andros."

"Andros disappeared more than three years ago. You can't be him unless…. What happened?"

"I got into a shootout with the feds. Ricky took a head shot. He was gone. I took a chest shot and went down. They put me in a hospital but I didn't make it."

"No, what happened to me? Does that mean I'm dead?"

"Fraid so, pal. Actually, I'm kinda glad you're here. Been by myself the whole time. I don't know how this is supposed to work, but being alone in this non-world is the shits."

"You mean there's no streets of gold or burning hell?"

"Naw, that Sunday school shit was all a lie. Haven't seen God either."

"Where are we?"

"We're nowhere, man."

"We thought the cops snatched you. I came back from Albuquerque to take over."

"The cops did snatch me. What happened since I've been gone? How long has it been?"

"You disappeared nearly four years ago. Things didn't go well. I'm not good in the first chair. We lost our drug connection for the H, then we lost the source of speed from Mexico. Sean's gun deal fell through after the first shipment. We did pick up some people smuggling, but not a lot. We were scraping by on the repair shop and the girls. Then Sean came back."

"What happened to him? He was in Afghanistan with the army. He was supposed to set things up."

"I guess CID got too close. They didn't have enough evidence to court-martial him, but they forced him to resign his commission. I was glad to see him. Things started to pick up right away. He got drugs flowing and had contacts to get us some guns, then the war happened."

"War! What war?"

"The U. S. got attacked. Not in the usual invasion sense. Somebody hacked into the electrical grid. Power went off around the country. It's still off in large parts. Then a bio-attack happened with smallpox."

"Jesus!"

"Yeah, Salt Lake City lost power for a while, and they quarantined the city. Actually a lot of the state, put up barricades to keep out the smallpox. Vaccine showed up about six months later. Life was nearly normal, except our business was in the toilet. Drug market went to zero and guns were blocked at the barricades. Business fell off for the girls and no people smuggling. We were starving."

"What did you do?"

"Sean heard reports that California was devastated. Smallpox wiped out more than half of the population, the power was still off. People rioted, attacked the capital, and city halls around the state. A lot of the cities burned. The National Guard got called out, but they were weak due to the smallpox. Police headquarters got ransacked and torched. The government was falling apart. Sean had this idea to move us there. We hit vaccine stations and hijacked a truckload."

"With nothing in Salt Lake, it was a smart move. It's what I would have done."

"Yeah, it was smart. We started off selling vaccine. When it ran out, we stole more. Pretty soon, the vaccine centers closed, so we sold fake vaccine. Money became worthless. You couldn't eat it and it wouldn't keep you warm. There were plenty of empty houses, but food was running out. Sean started organizing. If people signed loyalty oaths, he'd get them food."

"And the government just let him do that?"

"At first they sent in the army. They'd attack, take over territory, but they couldn't hold it. I guess with the problems across the whole country they didn't have enough troops. After six months, they withdrew and set up a perimeter isolating California."

"Fuckin' a! So you had the whole state?" Nick said into the mic.

"Not really. The Mexican cartel came up through Tijuana and held everything south of Los Angles and parts along the coast up to Ventura. Northern California belonged to the Chinese gangs. Vietnamese gangs held the middle part. The Russians tried to come in, but we killed most of them. What a bloody mess. Sean tried to pull everything together. He set up a summit to establish territories and get a truce. Sean's trying to build a new country while the U. S. is still weak."

"Sean always did have visions of grandeur, even when we were kids. So he's gonna make a new country with us in charge. Government always will be the biggest and strongest gang. If I had a hat, I'd take it off to him."

"Yeah, well our summit got attacked by a couple of snipers. Made a mess of it. Sean thought it was this bitch super sniper from Afghanistan. He put a big price on her head. After the attack, she disappeared. She was from Marana. We checked that out, but it was a zero. Her husband lived in Casa Grande so here we are, er were."

"If you got killed, then I guess maybe you were right."

"For all the good that info does. Sean's setting up another summit at the Community Center in Ventura. I'm not sure when, but he wanted this sniper taken out before that. Are we ghosts? Can we do anything?"

Nick said nothing. His mind turned over what he'd heard. Perhaps another hour questioning to confirm things then it was time to put Max back to sleep. During the hours he'd been at this, Ron had left and Kiki had come and gone, gone at the moment. Nick had been so focused he was surprised to see he was alone with the chamber. He asked his questions.

Exhausted, he heard Max calling from the chamber.

"Andros, you there? Andros?" Max's voice rose. His heartbeat increased. "Andros, don't leave me alone, man! I don't know what to do," he wailed.

Nick shook his head as he increased the sedatives and backed off everything else but the curanine. Max's voice trailed off.

The room was silent. It was only he and Max, alone with the black chamber dividing two worlds. Nick on the outside and able to leave and go out into reality. Max in another world able to go nowhere. What would be his reaction when he found out his death was a hoax to milk his brain? He had come to terms with being dead, and now he wasn't. All others he'd interrogated with the chamber were in institutions, insane.

He glanced at the black chamber and shivered.

Chapter Thirty-Seven

"Nick, are you all right?" asked Kiki as he came out of the chamber room. He nodded.

"Yeah, long session. Did you hear Max say Sean is planning another summit?"

"Looks like we may go back sooner than we thought." She shook her head. "I called the house and talked to Tama, told her we wouldn't be back for another day."

"They're doing okay?"

"Fine," said Kiki. "Nick, we need to get someone to train them besides us, especially if we have to go back now."

"K, I still don't like them going back into that hellhole of Los Angeles. Rosa's older. We could take her back if she'd go. I wouldn't feel as bad about that."

"We'll ask her. She has knowledge about the Hijos occupation that will be helpful, but the kids know about the Cs and the areas they took over. Nick, we've been through this. What are our alternatives?"

Nick pressed his lips together. "Regardless if the kids go back or not, I do agree about further training. We don't have time to teach them everything they'll need."

"Should we talk to Ron about a getting a military instructor?" asked Kiki.

"We can do that, but I'm not anxious to bring in someone else. The more people aware of us, the greater the risk we'll be betrayed. Let's call Brad, too."

Ron came back from the cockpit. "I informed the president that we had information Sean is moving to unify the gangs of California with a summit planned within a week. As you know, the president has agreed not to interfere with Sean's movement in return for the gangs not expanding beyond the California border and keeping the military bases as U. S. territory."

"What does he want us to do?" asked Nick.

"He still doesn't know about you and our efforts in California. We've kept it from him. He did say that things are improving on the east coast, and he's hoping to free up resources to take back California in a year."

A year, thought Nick. They had to keep Sean from declaring California a new country. If he was able to do that, and got recognition from other countries, military action by the United States could be construed as an invasion. How different would that situation be from China and Taiwan?

Nick pulled his mind onto another topic. "What's happening overseas with China and Russia?"

Ron smiled. "That's one bright spot, at least for now. China has not been able to unify. There is a chance it could drift back into warlord-held territories. We're watching one man, General Kai. He's the strongman in the military. The question is who will recover first, us or China? So, we're watching closely."

And what would we do about it? wondered Nick.

Ron continued, "Russia is in disarray. Vladimirov was assassinated two weeks ago. There is a battle raging within the military for control. Smallpox hit Moscow hard. The infection has been traced back to the week of Vladimirov's big speech, so the government leadership was all there. Only a few were vaccinated at the time. News has been spotty, but we estimate two-thirds of Moscow's population died."

Nick sighed and looked down. *Christ! The death of more innocents laid at the door of this whole war.*

Ron smiled, "Much of the military was deployed from the European invasion force and sent to counter China's invasion of the oil fields. Both Russian and Chinese troops were infected. Russia's no longer a world power."

"So what does that mean for the U. S.?" asked Nick.

"It means the two greatest foreign threats are gone for now," said Ron.

Though the news was a bright spot, the looming return to California dampened any joy within Nick.

"Ron," said Kiki, "We need to get training for the kids. They are not ready to return on the next trip, but we will need them to mount meaningful resistance afterward."

"Kiki, I'm still not sold on sending them," said Ron.

Nick watched this exchange. *Keeping* the kids from going back might be a greater problem. Tama, Joel and OJ were eager to return. After surviving the ruin of Los Angles, seeing the destruction of their lives, they wanted to wreak revenge on the Cs. They would find a way with or without Nick and Kiki's help. They had scores to settle. He could not blame them. "Let's table this for now." Kiki gave him a sharp look. "K, we'll figure this out. I'm too tired right now. Besides, I have another interrogation to go." Her face softened. This wasn't over.

"We'll help you get Max out of the chamber," said Ron. "You put him under and we'll send him to Ft. Huachuca for holding until we can move both Roberto and him to a more permanent facility."

Chapter Thirty-Eight

Loading Roberto into the chamber was a lot easier than Max. Roberto weighed half as much. Nick made the connections to monitor him and introduced the medications as needed. As Roberto awoke into the isolation chamber, separated from this world, his heart rate and breathing sped up. He was in a place with no light, no sound, no sense of touch. His mind floated in a void.

"Hello? Anybody there?" he asked in Spanish.

Nick said nothing. The chamber had sound deadening technology. He couldn't even hear his own voice.

"Where am I," he shouted.

"Roberto, you are with me." Nick's voice in formal Spanish transmitted directly into Roberto's head through the bone speaker.

"Who are you?"

"You know who I am. I am your God. The God you worshipped as a child and forsook as an adult."

Roberto wailed. "I am dead?"

"You have left your world and are with me."

"Now you come to me? You did nothing for me before."

"It is not for me to do for you. It is for you to do for me. You did not."

Roberto let out a sob. "How did I die?"

"What do you remember?"

"Me and Max were in this restaurant getting lunch. This cop come in. He talk and leave. Then he return. A man and a woman come in behind us. They shoot us."

"Why did they shoot you?"

"I don't know. We did nothing."

"Why were you there?"

"We were looking for this *asesinada* who killed some of our people in Los Angles."

"Did you find her?"

"The place we eat had her husband's name, Sabino. We think they are related. But now we never know. What is going to happen to me?"

"What happens depends on you. You must confess your sins to me—all your sins. You must show remorse for committing those sins so they can be forgiven. Only then can you go to heaven. If you do not, you will burn in hell for eternity."

Roberto moaned. "I have not confessed my sins for a long time. What if I forget?"

"Start with your most recent memories. Retrace your life. What do you remember? Tell me of the day before the restaurant."

"Yesterday, right?"

"Time has no meaning in this place."

Roberto wailed, "But we didn't do nothing to those people. They killed us for nothing."

"And you have never killed for no reason?"

Roberto was silent. "I have done evil things," he murmured.

"Tell me about Hijos de Hades."

"I joined them when I was a boy, spotting for them. They became my family. We took care of each other. With them I was somebody."

"You committed sins for them."

"Sí. But I had to. If I don't do that, they kill me."

"This was in Mexico?"

"Sí. I live in Mexico. Then I was sent to California with other soldiers."

"Tell me of the sins you committed in California."

"We go there after the attack on the Yanques. Hijos has chapters there. They were dying like everybody else so we stole the vaccine to give our *hermanos*. There was no law, so we took over. Our drug business died with all the people, except for the vaccine. We had a lot, but when that ran out we sold fake vaccine. People smuggling became our big business."

"People still wanted to go to the United States?"

"No. They want to get out. We smuggle them into Mexico."

"And you killed people, enslaved people, robbed people."

"Sí. But they were just little people. The men we kill or make slaves of. The women, we use them."

"What about the children?"

"Sometimes we do nothing and they die."

"I hear no remorse for these sins."

"I had to do it. It is part of the Hijos' plan to take back California. Everybody must be with us or they must die."

"What about Charon's Children?"

"Four years ago, we have a business with them. We get heroin from the Arabs and the Charon's Children kill people in the United States. We pay them with the heroin. They also sell the speed we make in the United States. But in California, we had our own people who distribute. Then those putas betray us. The police kill the Arabs in the U. S. and raid us in Mexico. They arrest our jefe, Julio Cardenas, but he escape."

Nick and Kiki looked at each other.

"Ah, Julio Cardenas?"

"Sí. He took over the Sinaloa cartel. He is now the biggest jefe in Mexico. He is working with *El Presidente.*"

Nick and Kiki had helped Julio escape from terminal interrogation. He had helped them return to the U. S. Now, it was coming full circle. He was the face behind a much larger Los Hijos de Hades.

"Charon's Children are leading the gangs in California under Sean Gallen."

"The Charon's Children only think they are in charge. We will allow them to unite all the gangs in their summit meeting next week."

"Then you will kill their leader, Sean Gallen, commit another murder."

"Or maybe we will let this assassin do it. That is why I am with Max. If he can work with us in charge, he will live. I will decide about the assassin when we catch up with her."

"You are no longer in that world. You will never catch up with her."

"I am not the only one. More will come for her. They do not stop."

Nick glanced at Kiki. She was frozen, her mouth open, eyes wide.

Roberto shouted, "California was stolen from Mexico. It will come back. Julio Cardenas is with our army in San Diego awaiting our move. He will lead us and we will have California as our country."

"I hear only pride from you. No remorse for those you killed or hurt. You cannot even see these people you destroyed. They were only roadblocks. Worse, you have replaced me, your god, with greed and your gang, Hijos de Hades. Eternity in hell awaits. Your soul is lost."

"Nooooooo!" screamed Roberto.

Chapter Thirty-Nine

"This puts a different slant on California," said Ron. "What was a domestic rebellion is now an invasion by a foreign power. We have to inform the president."

"What do you think he'll do?" asked Kiki. "He had an agreement with Gallen not to bring in troops."

"As long as Gallen is in charge, that agreement will hold," confirmed Ron.

"And when Gallen is gone?" asked Kiki.

"No agreement," stated Ron.

"I'm feeling a little used here." Kiki frowned. You want me to kill Gallen, President Davidson wouldn't mind, and the Mexicans want me to kill him."

"Yeah," said Ron, "the timelines are about the same for all of us. You forgot to add you want him dead for your own reasons."

"Yeah, I do," confirmed Kiki. "We need to get back to Casa Grande to get our gear together and make arrangements for the kids. Nick talked to Brad about a trainer. He suggested Johnny Cano, one of his deputies, ex-drill instructor, ex-Albuquerque detective. He knows some of our history."

"And you trust him?" asked Ron.

"Actually, we've never met him face-to-face. Talked to him during the terrorist attack four years ago. He was part of the team investigating the murders."

Ron looked wary. "We'll vet him and let you know if we find anything. Call me tonight. I'll take care of these two," said Ron looking at the gurneys. "Nick, can you keep them out for a twelve hour flight?"

Nick nodded.

***

"Kiki, you don't have to kill Sean. Let the Mexicans do it," said Nick. She was turned away from him, watching the Arizona desert roll by as they drove back to Casa Grande. Kiki remained silent. "If we can disrupt the summit, that's all we have to do," Nick added.

"It's a bit more complicated than that, Nick. First, I want to be the one to punch his ticket," she said through clenched teeth. "He's tried to kill me several times. He put a bounty on me that buys loyalty from most people. He was part of the murder of my parents. That being said, the Mexicans want him to pull a coalition together so they can take over. If that fails, they would have to do it, and the northern gangs would resist joining a foreign power, especially if it became known that Hijos killed Gallen. But if the alliance is already in place, they'd probably go along, at least until Hijos cements agreements together under their leadership. Once Hijos and the Mexicans take over, the military bases would be a question. Would you allow foreign bases in your territory? I wouldn't."

"They might. It would be like Guantanamo and Cuba."

"That only worked because we got our secretive asses kicked at Bay of Pigs," she snorted.

"If Julio Cardenas is in charge, we may be able to bargain with him. We did save his life," offered Nick.

"Bargain for what, Nick? The only bargain he could make would be the price he would pay for me to kill Gallen. It's a clean way to get rid of him and bring everybody together. Where does that leave me? With a higher price on my head, that's where."

"Yeah, I see what you mean. If you kill him before the coalition, then whoever tries to put it together might not forgive and forget. If you do it afterward, you're a liability."

"There is no right move here" sighed Kiki.

Chapter Forty

Rosa and the kids were seated at the table in the dining room of the Sabino household watching Nick and Kiki talk with a tall well-built man in a sheriff deputy's uniform on the patio. The late afternoon sun made it difficult to see any detail of the stranger, but their conversation had gone on for more than thirty minutes. At last Nick and Kiki came in, leaving the dark haired deputy outside.

With Kiki standing to one side, Nick addressed them. "K and I have to go back to LA. Things are happening with the gangs there. While we're gone, we've arranged for an ex-drill instructor to take over your training."

"Why can't we go back with you?" asked Tama.

"We must have you trained before we take you back" said Kiki.

"Trained!" snapped OJ. "We were fine there before you came."

"But you were just surviving," pointed out Kiki, "and only barely," she added, her voice harsher than she intended. "We have to go back to fight. That requires training and skills we're trying to help you develop."

"Why can't you do that?" asked OJ. "Why do we need a drill instructor?" He looked at Tama and Joel for support. "We did fine before you came."

"A drill instructor will teach you things faster and better than we can. Besides, we need to continue your training while we're gone," said Nick.

"How long will you be gone?" asked Joel, his voice quiet.

"We've learned that the Cs have another conference planned in Ventura in a few days. We're going back to keep that from happening. Rosa knows Ventura, so we want her to go with us." Nick glanced at Rosa. She nodded agreement. "We should be gone less than a week." The faces of the kids showed their displeasure at being left behind. OJ was about to object further.

"I'd like to introduce you to Officer Johnny Cano," said Nick." He was a Marine Drill Instructor and we've asked for his help." Kiki went to the patio door and opened it for him to come in.

The kids' eyes followed him as he entered. "Officer Cano, this is Tama, Joel and OJ. They will be your trainees." Nick stepped aside so Cano could address them.

He faced them, hands clasped behind his back. "First, I understand you have been through rough times. Nick and Kiki have brought you here to prepare you to return and take back your city. I'm here to help you do that." He stared at each face in turn. "We'll focus on weapons, explosives, first aid, hygiene, communications, and reconnaissance. These are basic skills you will need for this mission. Your training will be intense. I expect one hundred and ten percent effort from you. No whining, crying or sniveling." You're past that stage. From now on, you will address me as DI Cano." His voice was sharp, leaving no room for objection or discussion. The kids' mouths dropped open at this direct no-nonsense attitude. Their fear of him was obvious.

"Tomorrow you will travel to your new home. Pack essentials, no more than will fit in a backpack. I suggest you get to bed." It was not a suggestion at all. Their mouths snapped shut. "Now," he barked.

Nick watched the kids' faces as they scrambled for the bedrooms. Rosa followed to help. They went out on the patio. "What do you think?" asked Nick.

"OJ's impulsive. He'll need to learn control. Joel seems nervous, not sure of himself. He'll need confidence. Tama is cool and calculating–sniper material." Kiki nodded at his assessment. "I'll do the best I can," he continued. "Tomorrow Rosa, Monica and I will get the gear together we're going to need. We'll be shopping for provisions, too. How long do I have with them?"

"At least a month," said Nick, "maybe two months or more. We'll know more after we get back."

"Nick, Katherine, I owe you a beer from Albuquerque," said Cano. "I pay my debts"

"I'll get the beers this time," said Kiki.

The night was pleasant, sparkling stars overhead, a glow to the west where the sun had set. After Kiki passed out the beers, they clinked bottle necks.

"Thank you for settling the score with the scumbags in Albuquerque four years ago. Josh Edelston, one of the cops killed and beheaded, was my wife's brother. Our marriage didn't survive her losing her only brother. There's more, but…Our breakup is one reason I came back here. New start, you know."

Nick and Kiki nodded. They knew about new starts.

"I know very little of your story," continued Cano. "We were pretty sure you were behind the deaths of Ricardo and Joaquin de Silva." The unasked question was met with silence. Nick and Kiki smiled but said nothing. "After the FBI and Homeland Security moved in, us locals were put on other cases. We kept getting intel about gang activity that allowed us to make some big busts." Again his eyebrows raised in a questioning expression. Smiles but no answers were their reply. "You guys were the toast of lots of rounds at the bars. Rumors got pretty wild. I'd like to know the real story."

"Get the kids trained and we'll share over margaritas," said Nick.

"The kids, yeah." Johnny let out a sigh. "My son is about Joel's age by now. When we split up, my wife took him back to California. No word of them since the attacks. I can only hope...." he choked out, eyes teary. The silence hung in the air.

Not a story he was ready to share, thought Nick.

Johnny took a breath. "The Sheriff hasn't filled me in on much, said you'd explain."

Rosa came out to join them. "The niños are in bed. They are excited about the training, scared of you," she looked at Johnny. "They're upset that you," she looked first at Kiki then Nick, "are deserting them."

"We'll talk to them in the morning," said Nick. "Are you still all right with going back to Ventura?"

"Sí. I must."

Nick turned back to Johnny. "We have to prevent Charon's Children and Hijos de Hades from uniting California into another nation. We're buying time until the U. S. has the resources to go back. Having come from Ventura, Rosa can help us. This is a short term solution. The longer mission is to mount a resistance force. That's where the kids come in. They lived in the hellhole that is greater Los Angeles since the attack. They know the area, the streets and how to survive. They know others who can join us."

"Johnny," said Kiki, "what you cannot reveal to anyone is anything about Nick or me. Sean Gallen, the leader of Charon's Children, put a price on my head high enough to turn almost anyone. As of right now, very few people know about us. You join that exclusive club."

Johnny had a puzzled expression on his face. "Why is Sheriff Tierman involved?"

"Brad and I grew up together," stated Nick. "You were his recommendation to help us. I trust Brad. And we need your help."

"Who will I be working for?" asked Johnny.

"You'll have the same boss we do," said Nick, "the U. S. government."

"How are you going to keep all of this secret?" He held up his hands as if holding a great ball.

"When does this start? Where will I train these kid soldiers?"

He's agreed to help, thought Nick. "Tomorrow afternoon you, Rosa and Monica go down to the air park. The guard will direct you to our camp," said Nick. "Send me a list of whatever you think you and the kids will need. The next day, we'll drive down to Pinal Air Park using my brother's truck. Unused isolated facilities are where you and the kids will stay and train. Monica is going to take over the meals, laundry and cleanup for you."

"Johnny," offered Kiki, "we'll stay with you as long as we can. Then we have to leave. I know you were Recon in the Marines. You have to teach the kids as much of your skills as you can. Nick and I have worked with them in small arms, but they need a professional."

Johnny nodded, his hand on his chin. He looked at Kiki. "Kiki Russell, Katherine Russell?" She nodded. "Yeah, I know you now. I was out of the Corps while you were in the Sandbox, but I heard about you. Now I really want to hear the whole story of what happened. That's the deal, I'll do what you ask, but you have to tell me everything."

"You going to write a book?" asked Kiki.

"I always wanted to be a writer," he laughed. "Somehow, I don't think it'd be allowed."

Kiki smiled. "Ron Carson would be the one to decide what could be written."

"Government Grand Poobah Ron Carson?" Johnny's voice rose.

"Yeah. How we got tied up with him is part of the story. He'll be your contact for anything you need."

Nick watched Johnny's reaction. He was swimming with some big fish now. They were counting on him. Their lives depended on him.

Chapter Forty-One

Bing approached the southern barricade into Casa Grande on the Chuichu road. To break the trip from LA, he'd stayed in Mexicali overnight, making today's leg long and tiring. A uniformed sentry stepped out of a guard shack as he slowed his bike.

"Where you going?" asked the deputy, his voice not cold, but not friendly.

"Passing through on my way to Phoenix." He smiled. "Trying to catch up with some friends who came this way a few days ago. You seen a couple of guys on bikes?"

"Yeah, they came through, stopped for some eats," the deputy said, not smiling "Don't believe they're still here."

"I could use some eats and a seat that's not vibrating."

"Go ahead. There're plenty of places here."

As Bing rolled away, the deputy spoke into his radio. "Sheriff, got another biker coming into town. He asked about the other two."

"Okay, thanks," said Sheriff Brad Tierman. "We'll keep an eye on him."

Brad called Nick. "Another biker's in town asking about the others. What do you want to do?"

"We'll come down. Let's just watch him for now."

Bing drove around for a few minutes before pulling into the parking lot of the *Cocino de Sabino* Restaurant. Something about the name seemed familiar, but he couldn't put a finger on it. This early in the afternoon, the dining room was empty. "Sit wherever you want," came a female voice from the back. "I'll be with you in a minute."

Bing picked a table away from the window and sat with his back to the wall. A woman approached his table with a glass of water and a menu. She was brunette, short with dark complexion. Her hair was bobbed, brushed back.

"You want anything to drink beside water?"

"Yeah, gimme a draft, Bud if you got it."

"Got a local, but no Bud."

"Okay, I'll take that."

She handed him the menu. "Special today is green chili chiliquilas. Comes with rice and beans."

"Sounds good, but let me look for a minute." She left.

God, he was starving. What he really wanted was a steak. There it was–T-bone with sides and everything!

The waitress returned with his beer. "You ready?"

"Yeah. I'll take the T-bone, medium rare with baked potato and salad. Ranch dressing."

"You got it." She walked back to the kitchen.

He hadn't had a steak in years. California didn't have beef anymore, he was sure. At least not for the likes of him. Lots of soy and sprouts though. Shit, this was great! Cautiously, he tasted his beer. Wow. Better flavor than Bud. He was batting a thousand. The beer disappeared in no time. The waitress was back.

"Want another?"

"Yeah. Say, a couple of my friends came through here a few days ago. Did you see them?"

She half-closed her eyes as if thinking. "Big guy, shaggy with a beard and smaller guy, looked Mexican, both on bikes?"

"Yeah, that's them."

"They stopped in. One got the special, the other had a hamburger with fries. Said they were on their way to Phoenix. They were only here about an hour."

"They didn't stay?" asked Bing, hopefully.

"Don't think so. Check at the gate going out to the freeway. They log everybody going in or out. I'll get that beer for you."

So they'd struck out here. Okay, on to Phoenix. Might as well enjoy the steak.

In the kitchen, Kiki spoke to Nick and Brad. "It would be best if he passes through. If he disappears here, it will raise red flags."

"Right," said Brad. "I'll call the gate with the story."

"You make a pretty good waitress," kidded Nick. "A new career awaits."

Kiki punched him in the shoulder. "We got to get ready to head to the air park, help Johnny set up. Brad can handle things here."

It was starting again, serious shit. This dampened the mood. Her jaw tightened.

Chapter Forty-Two

Zero-dark-thirty, thought Nick as he guided the suburban along Interstate 10 toward Pinal Air Park. The kids were embarking on a path he disagreed with but one of necessity. He and Kiki were going back into harm's way. The pain and empathy he felt when she had been wounded was a sharp jab in his chest. He would not let that happen again.

He glanced at the rearview mirror. Joel stared out into the darkness outside the window. Nick knew he was torn. He didn't want to abandon his friends, but he didn't want to train to return to LA.

OJ's head nodded as he fought sleep. He was so young, not understanding the true nature of the training they were to go through. The long-term effect of being a soldier at war created major trauma in adults. What would it do to a child? Nick remembered OJ's anger at not going with them to LA. It was really about being left behind, feeling abandoned. Tama was silent, but her face wore a slight smile, as if she wanted to get on with it.

The guard asked Nick for his identification while shining his light into the suburban. He pulled his radio mic over and spoke into it. He looked back at Nick. "Someone will be here to guide you. Park over there," he gestured to a wide spot inside the fence. Kiki and Stephan parked the truck behind them.

"DI Cano will be here in a few minutes," Nick spoke over his shoulder. "Stay in the car." He got out and walked to the truck.

"K, Cano's on his way. You doing okay?"

"Basic training's going to bring back old memories," she snorted. "Some good, some bad. Bet I don't get harassed now like before."

"At least this time I'll get to keep my hair," laughed Nick.

A few minutes later, a Humvee pulled up. Johnny Cano leaned out. "Follow me," he shouted in full DI mode and gave them no pleasantries. The lights of the base glowed dimly behind them. Brightening sky above the eastern horizon signaled that dawn was an hour away. Johnny's tail lights wove through the greasewood and cactus, sometimes obscured by the dust cloud he was raising.

"Are we there yet?" asked OJ from the back.

Nick laughed. "I don't know." Though it seemed they had driven for hours, the dash clock indicated it had been only twenty minutes. After a sharp turn, his headlights played across four unlit prefab buildings. Johnny's brake lights flashed. They were there wherever there was.

Johnny strode up to them. "Women there," he pointed at one building. "Men there," he pointed at another. "Nick and Kiki, you're in that building with me. Carry your gear in, find your bunk. Lights are solar. When the batteries are dead, you're in the dark. Don't leave the lights on. We muster in that building in ten minutes. Get moving," he bellowed.

"Johnny, we'll be able to stay for a couple of days before we have to go back to LA," said Nick after they entered their quarters.

"I understand. How long do I have with them?"

"That will depend on how successful we are."

"I won't ask what you'll be doing. No need to know. What a crazy world," signed Johnny. "I'm training kids for war."

"Train them well," said Kiki. "If you don't think they can cut it, tell us. More than just their lives will depend on it."

Chapter Forty-Three

Nick and Kiki sat at the table in the modular conference room recently installed in the bay of the C-130. Built like the interrogation room next door, it was soundproofed, but with internet and radio links for video conferencing. At the moment they were all dark. "How are your people handling intense basic training?" asked Ron.

"Johnny's hard on them," said Kiki. "They're up before the sun and collapse into their bunks at night. It was exhausting for me, and I understood what was coming. I can't imagine what it's like for them."

"Will they make it?" asked David Kennedy.

"I'm sure of it," answered Kiki.

Kennedy cleared his throat. "We put drones over LA to keep track of what's going on. Gallen rarely goes outside. When he does, he's surrounded. His boy who visited Casa Grande came back yesterday. We haven't seen Gallen at all today. No news wasn't good news. It may have spooked him. He's really taking precautions."

"That makes him a difficult target," said Kiki, determination in her voice.

"Katherine, the summit is your target," pointed out Ron Carson. "We can work around Gallen and still do that."

"K," began Nick, "we can get him later. You will get him later."

"Yeah, sure," she said sharply. "Let's see the close ups of the Community Center."

"Ron, Roberto said Julio Cardenas is running the gangs in San Diego," said Nick. "We may have some history with him."

"What!" exclaimed Ron Carson. "How?"

"When we escaped from the interrogation boat four years ago, we took the next victim slated for interrogation. That was Julio Cardenas, a drug lord picked up by contractors for the CIA," said Nick. He shrugged. "We dropped him off in Mexico."

"Two years ago when we returned to the U. S.," said Kiki, "he helped us enter the US. At that time we didn't know if we'd be arrested or not. Look, we don't know if the Julio Cardenas in San Diego is the same one we saved."

"Where are you going with this?" asked Kennedy. "What would happen if you contacted him?"

"I'm not sure," said Nick. "We just wanted this out in the open."

Kiki frowned. "He'd probably kill us after what we're going to do to his Ventura operation. He might take pity on us from past history and make it a quick death."

"Does he know you're a sniper?" asked Kennedy.

Nick and Kiki looked at each other. "We never mentioned it," said Kiki. "He doesn't know about our interrogations either. We took him before we'd started on him."

"In fact," said Nick, "all he really knows is that we rescued him from capture and returned him to Mexico."

"He did ask a few questions," said Kiki, "but respected our not talking about our past. He has secrets he doesn't talk about either. We didn't ask."

"Let's tuck that information away for now," said Kennedy. "What are we going to do?"

Kiki looked at the images on the monitor. Security had been beefed up around the arena. They'd never get in, much less get out. An attack there was suicide. She widened the viewing area. Buildings were labeled. One caught her eye. Residence, Miguel Sanchez. "Isn't Sanchez the Hijos leader for Ventura?"

Kennedy nodded.

She looked Nick. "We're going to have to take Rosa with us this trip."

Chapter Forty-Four

Sean Gallen paced around his office like a caged predator. "Go over your trip to Casa Grande and Phoenix again," he said to Bing.

"I tracked Max and Miguel to this restaurant in Casa Grande. The waitress remembered them, even what they ate. She said they left for Phoenix. I checked with the gate on the road to I-10. The guard who logged them through said they told him they were heading for Phoenix. The gate guard in Phoenix had no record of them." Bing's gaze followed Sean as he paced.

"So," said Sean, rubbing his stubbly chin, "either they entered Phoenix unregistered or they never made it. Or they never left Casa Grande."

That thought troubled him. It would mean that the authorities were helping Russell. Since Bing's return with no news, Sean hadn't gone outside. He knew Katherine Russell was out there waiting for him. Frustration overtook him and he rampaged around the office, throwing things against the wall, taking little satisfaction as they disintegrated. As his screams reached a howl echoing down the hallway, Bing wisely left.

When calm enough to speak, he radioed Sanchez. "I get him. Momento," came the answer.

"Hola. What's happening, Sean?"

"How are the preparations going for the summit? What are your security arrangements?"

"I have fifty of my best men in teams with dogs combing the arena now. I have roaming patrols securing the perimeter for 1500 meters around the site. Tonight we will double those patrols. Nothing will get through. Tonight I'm meeting my jefe, Julio Cardenas at my house to discuss our future in California. We are ready. Nothing will happen at the arena I assure you."

"Yeah, that sounds good." We thought we had our arena secure, thought Sean.

"What about you? What's your security for the trip here?"

"We're coming in force. I've pulled everybody for the caravan. I've had scouts out along the route making sure it's clear. We'll be there."

"Anything we can do for you?" asked Sanchez

"Just make sure everybody stays happy."

"Hasta manaña. Until tomorrow, my friend."

Sean wished he felt as secure as he sounded. He'd taken every precaution he could and maintain his image. Sure, it would be better to ride in an armored Humvee, but that was not for the leader of a motorcycle club. He missed his organizer Max. Max he could trust. God! What had happened to Max? Was he even alive? Just like Andros, here then gone. No word, nothing.

After this summit was over, he'd send teams to hunt that bitch Katherine Russell down. She was good, but one thing he'd learned from the Arabs in the Sandbox was, forget casualties, attack in mass and overwhelm. The enemy didn't have the patience for a prolonged siege. That's what he'd make this. But first he had to get this coalition put together. Focus, he told himself.

Chapter Forty-Five

Rosa was decked out and eye-popping gorgeous in a skintight black leotard with red six-inch heels and a red scarf around her waist. She strode toward the cliff-side mansion Sanchez called his own. A guard stepped into her path and looked her up and down.

"Miguel sent for me," she said, her hips swaying. The guard took a second glance.

"I haven't seen you for a while," rasped the guard.

She saw his desire and smiled at him. "I've been busy." His focus was so intent he didn't notice the figures covered in black slip behind and into the estate. Rosa held his attention a few seconds longer before moving past him. She felt his gaze as he watched her move away.

At the main entrance, the two guards opened the double doors for her to enter. As she walked through, her heels clicking on the marble floor, their attention was riveted on her ass. They never heard the cough of the silenced pistols spitting death. Two men on the balcony raised their machine pistols but collapsed before they could fire. Kiki went to the right, her soft shoes making not even a whisper. Nick turned to the left, equally quiet. Rosa stepped out of sight under the sweeping stairway.

Kiki eased the door to the security room open. In front of the guard were six monitors showing views of the rooms and grounds, but his eyes were glued to a soccer match. The announcer yelled "Gooooooooal." As the man's arms raised in celebration, she shot him in the back of the head. Kiki studied the monitors, noting the locations and the remaining guards. She counted six. A shadow crossed one monitor blocking her view. When she saw the room again, two bodies were sprawled on the floor. She left the security room heading for the office and communications center.

Again, she eased the door open. One man wore headphones and moved to music only he could hear. Another was bent over a radio. He never straightened up. The bobbing man heard only his music as her shot pierced his earpiece. Kiki met Nick in the main entry, their faces covered by the ski masks. Rosa joined them as they headed toward the library. Her heels clicked, the sound echoing. She turned the corner to the library and the two guards at the door broke out of their lethargy. Their hands moved away from their guns. She obviously carried no firearms.

Nick and Kiki stepped around the corner, firing before the guards could react. The three stood before the library. Kiki held up her hand, then extended fingers, counting. At the third finger, they opened the doors and stepped in. Two men were seated in large arm chairs, liquor glasses on the table before them. Rosa grabbed Nick's gun before he could react and strode up to one of the men. "Miguel, you bastardo. Do you remember me?" His eyes flicked from the gun pointed at his forehead to her. He stared hard at her face, then shrugged. The gun spat and one eye disappeared. He slid from the chain to the floor in a shapeless heap. Rosa walked toward the other figure, gun leveled at him.

"Stop!" exclaimed Kiki, stepping forward.

Rosa froze. She glanced from the man toward Kiki. Kiki stepped close to the man and removed her mask. "Julio, do you remember me?"

His eyes widened and his mouth dropped open. "Katherine. Yes, I remember you. Is that Nick in that other mask?" She nodded. "So you are this *Diabla* who Sean Gallen is hunting. It was you that Sean's man and Sanchez's man, Roberto sought." She nodded. "Is Roberto dead?" She shook her head. "Will I see him again? He is my cousin."

"He is not dead. Pray that you don't see him," said Kiki.

Julio glanced at Rosa, the gun still pointed at him. He looked back at Kiki. "You have saved my life twice."

"I will make it three times," said Kiki. "Take your men back to Mexico. Do it soon."

A look of puzzlement crossed Julio's face. "Roberto spoke of my plans?"

Kiki just looked at him. "Make no calls, contact no one for an hour. If you do not abide by this, I will hunt you down."

He nodded.

Swiftly, they moved to the back of the house and out onto the steep stairs that descended to the thin beach below where their hidden raft awaited. The electric motor was only a soft hum as they moved toward the sliver of moon on the horizon casting wiggly lines of light across the calm sea. Kiki glanced back once. Had she done the right thing? They would see.

Chapter Forty-Six

Sean Gallen and his entourage approached the barricade into Mexiland. The three-hundred pound guard stepped out, holding up his hand for them to stop. "No meeting," he said.

"What!" exclaimed Sean. "We have an important conference today."

"Not today," repeated the guard.

"Get Miguel Sanchez on the phone. I need to talk to him," snarled Sean.

"Miguel is dead. *Asesinatos* killed him and his guards last night. Julio Cardenas left before the sun come up. No meeting."

Sean froze. His mouth opened and a scream erupted. He spun, jumped on his bike and sped away, gravel and dust flying. *She had done him again.* Hatred exploded within him like a nuclear bomb. He pushed the bike faster, countryside whipping by. At wide open, he was topping 145 miles per hour. His vision was a blur from the force of the wind making his eyes water despite the goggles. *I gotta slow down or she won't have to kill me. I'll do myself.*

Sean eased back and his speed slackened. *Okay, bitch. I'm coming after you, your husband and his whole family. I'm going to erase you.*

The first of the other Cs caught up. "Boss, you alright?"

"No, I'm not fucking alright, but I have a plan."

His remaining leaders gathered in his office. *Jesus, I miss Max. He knew how to handle all this.* "We're going after that bitch Katherine Russell. Since Max and Roberto disappeared around Casa Grande, that's where we'll start our hunt."

"When do we leave?" asked Bing.

As much as his emotions cried out for instant gratification, his military intellect kicked in. "We need to plan this out, not go in one big group like an army or we'll be attacked. Air power could wipe us out.

"Start getting things together. Guns, ammo, food. Our first group will leave in a few days. We'll all take the Mexican route so surveillance doesn't pick us up going east. Hijos can help get us across the border in different places. Once across, we'll move north and come at the city from the different roads." He pointed at the map. "There are seven checkpoints. The other roads are blocked, but we can go around them.

"Are we leaving colors behind?" asked Bing.

"No. We're not going in disguise. We're going in force. I want her to know we're coming for her."

"How many are we taking?"

"Everybody we can spare. I'll call the Mexicans. They want revenge for Sanchez and the others. They'll join."

Sean looked at the faces around the office. Some were grim, others eager. "If we can get ten groups of ten, we'll be able to overwhelm the locals without much trouble at each checkpoint. Before they can call for help we'll ?? in their knickers."

Chapter Forty-Seven

"Good job!" exclaimed Secretary of the Interior, Ron Carson. "You sure stirred up a hornet's nest," Katherine, Nick and Rosa sat in the conference room in the belly of the C-130.

"The radio traffic we're hearing says the summit was cancelled," added Director of the CIA David Edwards. "Gallen won't be able to get another one together for months. Hopefully, the U. S. will return and take California back."

"Ron, there's something else," said Kiki. "Julio Cardenas was in the house."

"What! Did you kill him?" asked David.

"No. I told you we had history."

"History!" exclaimed David Edwards. "You had a chance to take out the head of the Mexican cartel invading California and you didn't do it?"

"Nope," Kiki shot back at him. "Instead, I made him an offer to take his men back to Mexico. It was one he couldn't refuse."

"And you think he'll do it?" asked Ron.

"I do," said Kiki, her lips in a tight smile. "I told him if he didn't I'd hunt him. He believed me." Kiki watched him as the impact sunk in.

"Okay, it's done now. It was your call. I respect that," said Ron. "You did your job. What happens, happens. We're going to take you back to Casa Grande. We need to get the guerrilla force started in preparation to retake California. That means completing the training for the kids."

The electric tension of the adrenaline wore off during the flight. Nick and Kiki slept. Unable to rest, Rosa walked around the cargo bay, inspecting and touching things. She rested her hand on the door to the room where the isolation chamber lay, then pulled it away quickly. Something was in there she didn't want to know about. The thump of the landing gear startled her, and she hurried to her seat.

Kiki and Nick awoke as the loading ramp dropped down. The plane was parked inside the hangar and their SUV was near the wall to one side.

Ron and David accompanied them as they walked toward the car.

"We'll be in touch if anything happens," said Ron. "Meanwhile keep me informed as the training continues." He turned to Rosa. "Thank you for your help. Is there anything I can do for you?"

"Kill those bastards in California," she said. Her stare was intense.

"We'll be doing that," said David Edwards. "In the meantime," he glanced at the three of them, "get your forces together. We'll monitor conditions to determine when it's best to go back."

"Thank you," Ron said.

Nick climbed behind the wheel, Kiki beside him and Rosa in the backseat. They drove out of the hangar and headed west, the rising sun at their back. Thirty minutes later, the mobile buildings of their training center came into view. As their wheels crunched on the dirt road, the door of the mess hall opened. OJ peeked out, saw them and ran for the braking car.

As Kiki stepped out, OJ wrapped his arms around her. The other kids gathered around, giving Nick and Kiki hugs.

Johnny came up. "Welcome to Camp Revenge." When Kiki's eyebrows rose, he added "They named it. LA went well?" he asked.

"Adequate," said Kiki. "The summit is delayed."

"Did you kill bad guys?" asked OJ.

Kiki nodded. Joel and Tama smiled at seeing them but said little. "How's the training going?"

"I'll let you decide. We're just sitting down to eat. Join us for the day."

At the mention of food, Kiki's stomach rumbled.

OJ clung to her as they walked into the mess hall.

"We're learning all kinds of neat stuff," stated OJ. "We're gonna go back and kill bad guys."

She felt a twinge.

Chapter Forty-Eight

Nick and Kiki fell into bed. It had been a long day following a long night following a long day. They were exhausted but talked, their minds winding down until they could sleep.

"The kids are doing well, even after only a few days," said Kiki.

"Yeah, Johnny's good. At this pace, we'll be ready to go back in four or five weeks."

"At least as ready as they can be," said Kiki. Her mind prickled, her mouth opened.

"Nice job in Ventura, Katherine."

She looked at Nick. His mind had picked up the message, too. "Leave us alone. We're too tired to deal with you right now."

"I will not be long. You created a banquet for me with Sean Gallen. In his anger, he has resolved to destroy you. This last escapade convinced him that to move forward with his plans, he must kill you first. The Mexicans are also angry, so they are teaming up with the group Sean is leading to come after you. When their leader was killed it became a blood feud. They are determined to erase any trace of you."

"The hunted wants to become the hunter," said Kiki. She gave Nick a grim smile. "He will find it's not so easy." She'd been hunted before.

"The Mexicans want revenge, and unlike Sean, their reward will not die out with their leader. They are coming for you

and anyone associated with you. Take heed. I wish you luck."

"This will never end, Nick. As long as I'm alive, I'm a threat to you and your family. If they find out about the kids, they'll be in danger. Once they figure out Brad helped, he'll become a target. I'm a liability to everyone I care about."

"K, we'll call Ron tomorrow and work it out."

"We have to plan something."

***

The training was standard military. They exercised in the morning, ate breakfast at the mess hall then the marched out to the shooting range for small arms practice. Kiki was gratified to see how well the kids handled it. Their shooting skill had improved, and their safety was automatic. Tama was using the 800 yard range and grouping well.

After shooting, they had instruction on camouflage followed by hide and evade. Johnny was good. The kids' attention was riveted on him. Lunch was burritos in the field, then they were issued paintball guns to practice the hide and evade. It was a great game and valuable lessons. More calisthenics then lessons on hygiene followed by first aid. Joel was a wiz at that. As the sun was setting, they marched back to camp. Monica had dinner prepared. Afterward, lessons in reading and writing and math. There was no escaping school. At lights out, they fell into bed, except for the rotating guard, each doing two hours guard duty.

"They've grown up," lamented Kiki.

"Joel and Tama are soldiers," confirmed Nick, "not that much younger than we were when we joined."

"OJ is the one who's lost his childhood," said Kiki. Her heart ached for what could never be regained.

***

Ron and David were in a black SUV outside their mess hall at dawn the next day. "Nick, Kiki, we need to talk. Let's get breakfast."

Johnny and the kids left for morning training. Rosa, Nick and Kiki sat at the table with the two men. Monica brought coffee and left to prepare their breakfast. The room smelled of bacon, eggs and toast.

"After we flew out yesterday to bring you back, Point Mugu radioed. They intercepted a message from Sean Gallen to the Ventura Mexicans." Ron looked at Kiki. "He's putting together a force to kill you and was asking if the Mexicans wanted to join. This morning, our drones picked up a large group of riders outside the LA convention hall."

"We knew they'd do something," said Kiki, looking at Nick.

"They went south," continued Ron, "crossing into Tijuana. One interesting point was that many of the cartel invaders in San Diego were also crossing into Mexico. We don't know if they are joining Sean or Cardenas is honoring his word."

"You got drones over them? asked Nick.

"Yeah. We're maintaining constant surveillance."

"How many men?" asked Nick.

"About a hundred were gathered at the convention center," said David.

"They must have depleted their forces in LA and Ventura," said Nick. "Who's watching the home front?"

"We're still assessing. Our first concern is what to do about this invasion force. We're recommending to the president to treat it as a military action."

"Gallen isn't stupid. He knows he cannot fight the U. S. military," said Ron. "He won't bring a large force across the border and be vulnerable to air and ground attack."

Kiki's lips compressed. "He'll split up into small groups, so many we won't be able to watch them all."

"That's what we thought, too," said David. "What we want to do is get the military minds involved and put together strategy."

Heads nodded around the table. "If we can get the military involved, it may be our avenue back into California," said Ron. "Let's conference with the president. I'll set it up."

Chapter Forty-Nine

"Before I get the president on the line, we need to have our story straight," said Ron, looking at the faces around the small table in the portable conference room. "The only ones who know about our activities in California are the four of us."

"And our LA refugees," said Kiki.

"The president knows nothing about them either. We cannot reveal the kids and our plans involving them," stated Ron.

"Better to seek forgiveness than permission," muttered Kiki.

"Exactly," exclaimed David.

"We have to tell him of our excursion into LA," said Kiki. "There's no other way to explain Sean's invasion force. Okay, Nick and I did that on our own. No U. S. help or knowledge. You and David didn't know."

"The president wouldn't hang us out, would he?" asked Nick.

"He's not that kind of man," stated Ron Carson. "He's not stupid either. Despite our claim of not knowing about you, he will wonder why you were there and how we found out about you."

"We were there to kill Sean Gallen because he has a price on my head!" spat Kiki.

Trying to calm her, David held up a hand. "He can accept that. He knows about Gallen's summit and attempts to unite California into another nation. By agreement, he won't interfere and Gallen's forces won't attack the military installations."

"A deal with the devil," snorted Kiki.

"I agree. Now the Mexicans are involved. How did that happen?" David's eyebrows rose at the question.

"Nick and I hit Ventura because Gallen was supposed to be there. He wasn't, but the Mexicans didn't understand we were only after Sean." That sounded weak even to her. "We had to defend ourselves. Let's make the call."

The connection took a few minutes. "Mr. President," opened Ron, "I'm with David Kennedy, Nick Sabino and Katherine Russell."

"Good to talk with you, Katherine and you, Nick, though I'm not sure I understand what this call's about. As you requested, Ron, I have General Tom Edwards, Chairman of the Joint Chiefs, and Secretary of State Sharon Volgyi with me."

"Sharon, Tom, good to talk to you again," said David Kennedy. "Without going into detail, the situation here in the Southwest is becoming fluid. Our drones have been following a large group of Charon's Children and Hijos de Hades who have entered Mexico. We believe they intend to travel east in Mexico and enter the U. S. across the southern border of Arizona."

The president gave a grunt. "Why would they want to enter the U. S.?"

"We believe they are after Katherine Russell. They intend to kill her."

"Why and why now?" asked Sharon Volgyi, an edge to her voice.

"Sir, as you know Gallen put a bounty on Katherine. She and Nick went into California to kill

Gallen. They missed but disrupted his unification plans."

"How convenient for us," said Volgyi sarcastically. "We had peace, a truce. The president and I worked hard to hammer this out."

They waited for the president to ask if they had backing or if David or Ron had knowledge of this attack. He didn't ask.

"When did this happen?" asked General Edwards.

"We attacked at the time of Gallen's first summit, sure he would be there," said Kiki. "He came late, but other gang leaders were killed. The summit didn't take place. That was three months ago."

"First summit?" asked the president. "How did you know about this summit?"

"We were in LA for a while," said Kiki. "It was on the street that he was holding a conference, seeking approval backing him for leader of the new nation. It was an opportunity for us."

"Of course he scheduled another," said the president.

"Yes, sir," said Kiki. "It was last week. Nick and I raided a house in Ventura where the Hijos de

Hades leadership was staying. We were sure Gallen would be there. He wasn't. There was a gun battle with the Mexicans. Several, including their Ventura leader, were killed. The summit was cancelled."

"I get the fact you want to kill Gallen," said Volgyi, "but you put our negotiations at risk for this personal vendetta."

Kiki's face twisted into a snarl as she started to respond. Nick put a hand on her arm. She looked down at it and pressed her lips together.

"So Gallen has decided he has to get rid of you so he can hold his summit and move ahead with his plans," Volgyi continued. "You knew we had negotiated a deal not to attack him."

"Yes, Madam Secretary. That is why Nick and I did this on our own." Her voice was overly formal and hard.

"And now Gallen is sending a force to take you out," said the president.

"Sir," said David Kennedy, "this invasion has that as an objective, but perhaps to also see how strong our forces and our resolve are. The question before us is how do we respond?"

"What's our timeframe?" asked the president.

"From Tijuana to the Arizona border is one day. From the border to Casa Grande is two hours. They could be in Casa Grande tomorrow if they travel all night. We're watching them and will refine our estimates over the next few hours."

"Tom, what do you think we should do?" asked the president.

"Mr. President, we have a National Guard unit on Interstate-8, two hours from Casa Grande. It's a small unit maintaining a roadblock to halt any California refugees carrying contagion from moving east out of the state. As the number of refugees has dropped dramatically and that threat has lessened, the forces have been reduced. Only fifteen troops are on site at any time. We've been rotating them in and out. The unit has some armor. We could reinforce the locals."

"Is that going to be enough? What else can we do?"

"We could turn these two over to them," said Sharon Volgyi. "Politically it's the best solution."

Kiki leaped up ready to attack. Ron muted the mic. "Not now, Katherine. Let's listen." Nick pulled her back into her seat.

"Whatever we decide, that option is not on the table," said the president firmly. "Tom, what do you think their plan is?"

"Gallen is ex-military. He'll run it as a military exercise. He'll split up his men and enter the city from numerous directions, causing us to divide our forces. Groups of ten can break through any single roadblock. Several questions need to be addressed. Can we stop them from entering the city? Some will get through, there is no wall. As a sub question, how far are we willing to go to stop them?" There was silence as that thought hung in the air.

"What are they going to do once inside?" continued Edwards. "Their goal is to find Katherine and kill or capture her. How do they do that? It won't take long to find out where the Sabino house is. So they will assault it. How defensible is it?"

"My father built that house with the idea of being able to secure it," said Nick. "It's on a hill overlooking Interstate-8. Behind it, the hill continues to rise another 100 feet. The driveway is the only vehicle access." He looked at Kiki, who nodded. "There are clear fields of fire from the hill covering the driveway. A ground assault could come up the hillside directly and over the mountain from the east."

"Are these guys motivated enough for a ground assault?" asked General Edwards.

"It certainly isn't their forte," answered Kiki. "What kind of bikes are you seeing from the drones?"

"Almost all are street bikes, only a few trail or dirt bikes," answered David.

"We're looking at Google Earth of the area," said the president.

"If I were Gallen," started General Edwards, "I'd send my dirt bikes over the hills to the east. Let them set up suppressing fire while the main force blasts up the driveway laying more suppressing fire as they advance."

"How do we counter that?" asked the president. "Could we lend air support?"

"It's too tight for planes, though gunships might work. We'll put our own people on the hills to the east and prevent them from using it," said General Edwards.

"Maybe some on top of the hill behind the house," said Kiki. "That should give a 360 degree observation point. We'll be able to spot anyone from there."

"That's long range shooting," observed the general.

Kiki chuckled. "But not too far. Outfit our guys with colored armbands and infrared beacons."

"Beacons?" questioned the president.

"If I were Gallen," said Kiki, "I'd do a night assault."

"I agree," said Edwards. "We have to be prepared for that."

"Can you get us night vision goggles and sights?" asked Kiki.

"We'll fly some in today," said the General.

The planning details continued, but Kiki was silent. *How many people would die for her?*

Chapter Fifty

"Sean," said Bing, "I find two addresses for Sabino in Casa Grande." Midafternoon and they were the only ones in the dining room at a hotel in Sonoyta, Sonora. The new head of Hijos de Hades Ventura Chapter, Joaquin Guzman, was with them. Overnighting here gave them a chance to plan things out. "One house is in the city, and listed for Stephen Sabino. The other is south of town on a hill, listed as the address of Dr. Michael Sabino."

"We'll hit them both." Sean's face held a satisfied grin. "Anybody associated with Sabino and Russell is erased. My bet is that the bitch and her husband are in the house on the hill. If she's not there, it won't matter. We'll kill everybody, put their heads on pikes. When she surfaces, we'll get her."

"Think they know we're coming?" asked Joaquin.

"If they're ready for us, then that bastard president's been lying to us. He's behind the attacks."

"You mean we'd be facing the U. S. Army?" asked Bing, worry in his voice.

"We're attacking tomorrow. They won't have time to bring in troops."

"What about air force?" Bing's voice whined. "Planes could wipe us out before we even get close."

"We're going to grab some women and kids to take with us. That'll stop any air assault. We'll split up in Ajo. You two will take half the guys to Gila Bend then head east to Casa Grande. Before you get there, split up into smaller groups. Put each group on a road into the city. They can't guard every road with enough people to stop us. Go to the house in town. Kill anybody there and burn the house to the ground. Go to the restaurant. Do the same. If you find that bitch, I want her alive."

"Where will you be, Boss?" asked Bing.

"I'll take my guys to the place on the hill. After you burn the house and the restaurant, meet me there."

Sean looked at the map again. It wouldn't be easy, and he'd lose guys for sure. He'd send men up the slopes, cover them from the hills to the east and west. Once they had everybody's heads down, they'd roar up the driveway in a typical advance and cover assault. The hostages would limit the defender's fire. The complication was Kiki the sniper. She was good, but she was only one person.

How many other people would be at the house? Would she even be there? Yeah, she would.

"Bing, Joaquin, circulate the word. We're going to leave here tomorrow afternoon. Guys can party, but I want them ready by three pm."

"Why so late, Boss?" asked Bing

"I don't want to spend any more time in the U. S. than we need. It'll be harder for them to defend in the dark, and better for us to escape. We'll send in scouts a couple of hours before we leave to get some idea of what we're facing. When you come in from the east and north scope out the roadblocks." He looked at the two men. "Send your guys in. If there's strong resistance shift to a weaker point, but keep up the pressure on all sites. Don't let them focus their resources. At the weakest one, punch through. Go directly to the Sabino house and the restaurant." Sean stood.

"Kill everyone and torch 'em. Soon as you're done, pull your forces and join me at the hill," he repeated. "You're going to lose guys. But you have to do the job. Got that?"

"Yeah. We'll gitter done," said Bing. They both nodded.

"How are our Hijos buddies doing on the trip?" He focused on Joaquin.

"We're showing our gringo amigos all the cool places." Joaquin smiled. "Some of us are going to the beach in Rocky Point. It's about an hour away. Lots of places to party there. Want to come? The chicas at Jua Jua's are special." A wide grin appeared through his bushy mustache.

"Go have some fun but don't get too wasted. Make sure nobody gets arrested." He pointed at Joaquin. "That's your job number one. You're in charge down there."

"Okay, Jefe."

"Be back here by noon. I want to look everybody over. We'll do a weapons check and briefing at two. I want this bitch alive. Whoever captures her alive gets fifty big ones. Dead, I'll kill 'em. Anybody missing or unable to make the trip, I'm holding you responsible. We leave at three. Got it?"

"Yes."

"Sí."

"See you tomorrow." Sean watched them leave. Russell was at that house. He felt it. He tasted it, but the sweet flavor he'd anticipated had a sour tang of fear.

Chapter Fifty-One

"Johnny, we need an emergency meeting. Assemble everyone in the mess hall. We'll be there in thirty minutes," Nick said to the drill instructor. The Pinal Air Park guard checked Nick's and Kiki's IDs and waved them through. As they pulled up to Camp Revenge, the door to the mess hall opened and OJ flew out.

"You're back! What's happening? DI Cano brought us here for a meeting."

Kiki laughed. "Let's go inside. I'll tell you everything." Once they were seated, Kiki's smile faded as she addressed the group. "Things moved faster than we thought. The Cs and the Hijos are coming to Casa Grande. We need you." OJ whooped as she watched the expression on Johnny's face. "Are they ready?"

His eyes locked on her. "I never thought any of my trainees were ready but that didn't mean they didn't go. I do feel better knowing they'll be in Casa Grande where I can keep an eye on them."

Kiki nodded. "The Cs and the Hijos will come after us at the Sabino house, We'll be a team guarding it. Mount up we leave in fifteen." The kids dashed out. Rosa paused then walked past Kiki.

Kiki's gaze returned to Johnny. "Take all the arms and ammo. Put suppressors on the rifles. Bring any desert cammo, too. This is going to get ugly."

"When you called, I was afraid of that." Johnny shook his head. "Why don't things ever go according to plan?"

"They are going according to plan, just not our plan."

On the drive back, Kiki's mind was rolling through setups and scenarios. Rosa and the kids were riding with Johnny so he could talk to them. He wanted to give them last minute instruction for this defensive action.

In the Sabino driveway, Kiki looked first at the hill behind the house, then to the hills to the east and finally out over the valley. "Nick, how many people will be here?"

"The Sabino family, Miriam, Stephen, Barb and the kids. I'll call Brad to see if he can send anyone." He turned away.

"Johnny, this won't be a siege. It'll be a hard and fast attack. They will try to overpower us right away." Nick nodded. "If it goes on too long, we'll get help from the town or Ron will move forces here. It'll be over one way or the other tonight."

"How many are coming?" he asked.

"The latest report is between fifty and seventy-five."

"Whew! That's a lot for us to take on."

"Gallen can't be sure where we are. Part of his forces will to go into the city. Our address here is no secret, but Stephen's is listed, too. He'll split up. We'll see about half of them at first. Once the forces are done with the city, they'll come here."

"Okay, so we have to inflict heavy causalities quickly to discourage them," said Johnny. "How much damage will it take for them to go away?"

"That is the question. The way I see it, the main assault has to come up the driveway from the north. Some will climb the slope on foot below the house.

We need snipers on that hill," Kiki pointed behind the house. "One covers the driveway and the front of the house. The other covers the hills to the east to keep any bad guys from flanking us or sniping at us. Each needs a spotter." Johnny nodded. "I want you up there with them. Lend help and cover them if anyone gets the idea to attack over the hill behind them." Johnny studied the hill, marking out positions.

"I'll be on the ridge to the west so I can cover the slope below the house and the driveway. Nick will be with me as spotter and cover my butt. If the hills to the east get dicey, I'll be able to help."

"Long range," said Johnny. "Be nice to have more than one spotter."

"Yeah, it would. Let's see how our deployment goes."

Johnny smiled. "I also brought Claymores. We can cover the driveway and the slopes if the traffic gets heavy."

Nick walked back. "Brad is putting his family with others in the high-school gym. They're putting a heavy cordon around it, including some of the light armor from the National Guard post. He says he can spare three guys. What do you want to do with them?"

"Give them armbands and IR markers. They can hold the hill to the east. They must watch the hill behind us so nobody comes in from the south."

"Where are you going to be?" asked Nick.

"You and I are going up there," she said, nodding at the ridge to the west. "We'll be covering the slope below the house."

Nick nodded.

"Okay. Johnny, who're our snipers? Who're our spotters?" asked Kiki. You know them better than we do."

"Tama and Rosa are the best shooters. That leaves OJ and Joel as spotters. So the teams are Tama and OJ taking the hills to the east and the front of the house. Rosa and Joel will cover the driveway and front of the house. We will need defenders shooting anybody who makes the patio wall."

"Miriam, Stephen and Barb have the house. Anything that comes over that wall, they shoot. Stephen knows how to use a gun. Mom keeps a 12 gage behind the door. It's not for show. We'll pull the railroad ties from the flower beds and make barricades for protection. Barb will supply ammo and water as needed and cover the kids."

"That sounds good. You need help with the barricades?"

Nick shook his head. "Stephen and I can handle it."

"Johnny, let's take the kids up the hill and find our shooting positions. Tama and Rosa are on the 25-06's, Joel and OJ are on the M-4's with binoculars. We'll have night vision. Johnny, pick what you want," Kiki said.

As they started their climb, Nick's phone rang.

"Hey, Nick, Ron here. How are things going there?"

"We're getting deployed, setting up our defenses."

"David and I are watching the group in Sonoyta. They're getting ready to cross the border. A couple of scouts left two hours ago. Have you seen anything of them?"

"We'll get someone on the hill and I'll call Brad," said Nick.

"Our guess is the main force will be there in two hours and set to assault in three. The National

Guard unit left Gila Bend two hours ago and should contact the sheriff any time."

"Okay, I'll call him. He promised us some men."

"Nick, if you can hold out for four or five hours," Ron offered, "we'll have a strike force on the ground."

"Thanks, Ron. I'm not sure it will last that long. Gallen knows that troops will be coming. If he doesn't take us in two hours, he'll withdraw."

"That's a good thing, right?"

"We need to end this. Our best chance is here, on our ground."

"The timing isn't ideal. Nick, we could take him in LA. We're only months away from going back. Just hold out until our forces get there."

"We will." There was no use saying more. "Keep us informed of their progress."

"Roger that. David and I are glued to the drone view."

"Thanks for the help. We'll see you in two days."

"K, we need to take a hike. Bring your rifle," said Nick, grabbing two pair of binoculars.

Chapter Fifty-Two

The hike to the top of the hill took twenty minutes. Nick and Kiki nestled in behind rocks and scanned the ChuiChu highway. That was the route the scouts would take.

"Driving Gallen and the Hijos away won't be enough. They will continue to hunt me and those I love. We have to stop this," she said, the binoculars to her eyes. "Killing Gallen may not be enough. The Cs may forget the bounty, but I doubt it. The Mexicans won't. Since Roberto will disappear, his uncle Julio Cardenas won't forget either. Family honor will demand revenge." She put the binoculars in her lap and looked at Nick.

"What are you suggesting, K?" *They had not thought past the next few weeks. The world was in too much turmoil. What was she suggesting?*

"I don't know, Nick, but I'm tired of this. I want it to stop." There were tears in her eyes. "Can we go back to the boat? Those were the golden years of my life." She peered through the binoculars again, masking her expression.

"K, we both loved it, but after three years banging around the Caribbean, we were bored." Nick lowered his glasses, stared at Kiki as she appeared to be intent on watching the road. "We left because it was time to come back."

"I understand, Nick, but look what we've come back to." She didn't or wouldn't look at him. "Here they come." Her voice had changed to the sniper-voice–Hard, cold, all business as she reached for her rifle. Everything was pushed aside as her total focus was on the targets.

The two bikes had stopped at an intersection. A dirt road led to the mountain they perched on. One bike turned off, the other continued north to I-8, entering and heading west.

Nick called Brad. "We just saw a bike head west on I-8. He's probably going to Stansfield to approach from the west, scouting the entrances to the city."

"Roger," came Brad's reply. "We'll get a reception committee ready for him."

Nick looked at the other biker. Stopped at the foot of the mountain, he eyed the formidable climb to the top, trying to pick a route. He stepped back to the bike, grabbed a rifle and a pack. With one last glance, he started up a faint path.

They watched.

Halfway up he paused, took a drink and pulled out his radio. His conversation was short. Whether it was to Gallen or the other scout, they didn't know.

The blast from Kiki's rifle caused Nick to jump. When he looked back, the biker had rolled a few feet down the mountain, coming to rest against a large rock. Spots of blood and gore covered the ground. He never knew what hit him. "Why didn't you shoot him at his bike? asked Nick.

"Then we'd have to go all the way down the mountain to get his radio," answered Kiki.

Her voice was matter of fact. No emotion. "I'll get it," said Nick rising and turning downhill. Kiki's revelation about wanting out, being tired of it all was troubling. He recognized it as a call for help, but he had no answer. They could go back to the boat, but that was a temporary solution.

Kiki's shot had torn away the back and spine of the C. His radio and rifle were sticky. Nick looked at his face, eyes wide open, mouth agape with a scream frozen in his throat. He was a kid, about Rosa's age.

By the time he got back, Kiki had their gear packed and was again searching the road below.

"The road's clear. We need to get everybody set up. Johnny can come here to watch for the arrival." She handed him his pack and pushed a button on her com unit. "Johnny, we're heading back. Threat's gone for now."

Chapter Fifty-Three

"Everybody set?" asked Kiki. She and Nick were on the ridge to the west of the house and had a clear view of the driveway and the slope from the valley up to the patio. "Check in."

"Tama and Joel set."

"Rosa and OJ set."

"Johnny, what about you?"

"I've got both sniper posts in view. They're cammoed up nicely. If I didn't know where to look, I couldn't find them. The road is still clear."

"Yeah, good. The C's radio is quiet. They're probably not in range yet," said Kiki.

"Guard unit one. Are you in position?"

"Yes, ma'am. We got eyes on all approaches. Nobody's getting up here."

"Eyes in the sky put the tangos on I-8, fifteen minutes out." Kiki paused "They also tell me the baddies are using hostages as shields. Stay frosty. Pick your shots. Keep in mind the Cs and the Hijos will kill the hostages anyway." She wasn't sure that last was true, but history said so. "When it's too dark to see well, don your night vision. Nobody gets through."

She desperately wanted to pick out Gallen and end this, but the bikers wore helmets. Impossible to find him. The first bike stopped halfway up the driveway. With an arm wrapped around a child, he started up. Yeah, it made sense to assault on foot rather than on the bikes. They couldn't shoot with one hand on a kid and the other on the bike. This might change if they decided to rush the house. Covering fire came from farther back, but they had no targets.

"Rosa, take the lead guy. The rest of you, take your targets of opportunity. Free to fire."

Kiki watched the biker's head explode as the high velocity bullet struck. The child broke free and scrambled for cover to one side of the road. "Nice shot."

Five figures approached, running with children and women in front of them. Kiki took the lead down as Rosa and Tama took two more. Kiki looked at the slope. Six men were climbing toward the wall. In rapid succession, three fell. The others turned to flee. One fell, another took a shot to the chest. She shot the third in the leg. The suppressed rifles weren't quiet, but the noise was from the bullets, making it difficult to locate the shooter.

"Tama, the ridge," she heard OJ say.

"It's okay," said Nick, his hand on her shoulder. "Tama and the guard are taking care of them."

For the moment, the slope was clear. More were coming up the drive, some on foot, some racing up on bikes, hoping speed would protect them. The bikes wove around. Kiki took the lead bike. It slued sideways and went down, pinning the hostage beneath. The driver lay still.

"Oh no!" cried Rosa. Her shot had passed through the hostage hitting the driver. Both lay unmoving.

"Pull it together," said Kiki. "We need you. Don't stop. Later is time enough for sorrow and regrets." She sighted on another biker. His chest exploded. The fallen bikes were acting as an obstacle course causing the rush to slow. Over the C's radio she heard Gallen move more men to the eastern ridge to suppress the deadly fire.

"Tama, watch the ridge. You guys to the east, expect more company. Yell if it gets heavy."

"Yes, Ma'am."

"Johnny, any activity?"

"Five bikes just pulled up. They're going to assault the ridge."

"Need help?"

"Not yet."

Two quick reports echoed from the west.

"Three left. They're having second thoughts," came the report over the radio.

"They're calling for help," said Kiki. "Take 'em if you can."

"Oh yeah. They're firing back, but it's wild, no idea where I am. If more arrive, I'll call."

Okay, thought Kiki. The backdoor was safe for now. She checked the slope below the patio. Six men were trying an advance and cover tactic. Without a target, it didn't work. Two men fled down the slope.

Nick tapped her shoulder. "Take a breath."

Kiki looked over the top of the rifle. It was growing dark. She hadn't noticed. "Time for night vision," she announced. "Turn on your IR blinkers so we know who's who."

Chapter Fifty-Four

"Boss, we're taking an awful lot of casualties," said Sam.

"I fucking know that!" shouted Sean, looking toward the city. Two orange glows lit the darkening skyline.

He called Joaquin and Bing. "How's it going? Good. Head over here." He glanced at Sam. "We'll have reinforcements shortly. It'll be dark soon," he said, looking up at the sky. "

The additional men arrived at a rally point out of sight of the house and hills. He called his lieutenants together. "How many losses did we take in town?"

Joaquin and Bing looked at each other. Bing frowned. "We lost fifteen between the checkpoints and the house. It was empty, but we burned it.

Same with the restaurant. The civilians are holed up in the high school gym. They have two tanks there, so we left it."

Sean nodded. *Yeah, that was okay.* He'd lost thirty men. That left thirty-five for the assault. *Should be a piece of cake.* He'd underestimated the capability of those at the house. *Where had those other shooters come from?* From his observation, there were four or five shooters. *Might be spotters with them.*

He turned to his men. "Send ten guys to that ridge to the east. Send ten more to the back side of this mountain to flank 'em. We have to suppress their fire. Keep their heads down. Under that cover, we'll charge up the driveway. Once we make that, we'll use the wall as cover to take out the snipers."

"What about the hostages?" asked Bing.

"Keep most of them down here. With the dark, they'd only get in the way." He shrugged. "We'll need them for the trip back to Mexico. Let's stop for a breather. Get water, take a piss, grab some food."

The bitch and her friends had been ready, so they were getting help, but no federal troops had arrived, no air support. Either the U. S. wasn't willing or wasn't capable of helping quickly. Sean had no doubt they would show up. He had to get this over.

Fatigue showed in the face of his guys. He had to rally them. "Joaquin, got your men ready to go?" The Hijo nodded. "Bing, you ready?" He nodded. Call me when you're in position. The men mounted up and roared off. Sean split his remaining force. Six would assault the house up the slope. He kept one back who would locate the shooters by their muzzle flashes. The rest would make a run up the driveway. He waited for the calls that his flankers were in position.

It seemed like forever until he got a call from the east hill. "We're taking fire. Lost three already."

"Shit! There can't be that many. Charge 'em. Bing, what's happening?"

"Shooters have us pinned down at the foot of the mountain. Of the five you sent before, four are down. I've lost four more."

"How many shooters?"

"We're seeing at least three flashes. Don't know if it's three shooters or one guy moving around. Whichever, I'm losing men. They obviously have night vision."

"Spread your men out. Advance one side then the other, sometimes simultaneously. Take that hill!"

"Yes, Boss."

Chapter Fifty-Five

"Tama, focus on the eastern ridge," Kiki radioed. "The guard will need your rifle. OJ, go up the hill and help guard the back door. Johnny, you get that message? Don't shoot him. Sean told them to charge. Pin them down until OJ gets there."

"Roger. Thanks."

"Tama, get to a place where you can't be seen from below. Get behind something solid between you and the house. We'll cover you while you move. They'll spot us and concentrate fire, so we'll keep moving."

"Roger, Kiki," came Tama's reply.

"Nick, you watch the slope and the drive. I'm going to move to another spot so I can help Tama and the guard." Kiki moved to a notch with a boulder between her and the house. She settled in, placing her scope on the ridge. The infrared flashers identified the guard. She watched men come over the ridge, three heading directly for the guard, two more on each side, flanking.

"Tama, take the two on the right." These were long shots, 800 yards for Kiki. She took a breath, held it and placed the glowing crosshairs over one man on the left. Her mind automatically calculated the lead and drop. She fired. Less than a second later, he fell. Already sighting in on the other man, she took a deep breath, let half out, squeezed. The rifle bucked against her shoulder. The man fell.

Kiki checked the three men who were in the center. Two were down from guard fire. The remaining man was charging the guard position, firing as he ran at them. She sighted on him. Bam, down. The men on the left had gone to ground. Tama hadn't hit them, but she forced them to seek cover, stopping their advance.

"I missed," apologized Tama.

"Don't worry. They won't be shooting at us." As she said this, bullets began hitting around her. Her position was compromised to those below. "I'm pinned, Nick. Give me some cover so I can get out of here." Under cover of his fire, she ran down the hill, ducking behind another rock. Bullets whistled overhead as they continued to shoot at her old position.

"K, we need to do something with the slope," warned Nick. At least six guys were scrambling upward toward the patio wall.

"Stephen, hit the Claymore," Kiki called. There was an explosion and the slope was obscured by dust. When it cleared, no people were standing. The bushes and cacti were shredded. It would be nice if they could use the Claymore set up on the driveway, but hostages were still there.

"How's the guard doing?" she asked.

"We still have a couple of tangos moving here, but their heads are down for the most part. Thank you, whoever is keeping them pinned."

Kiki turned her attention back to the driveway at the sound of roaring motorcycles. *Here they come.*

They had left the hostages behind, though there were still some trying to grow small on the sides of the road, seeking cover where there was little. Rosa took out the leader. Kiki took out another. One with a red helmet hung back. Her bet, that was Gallen. She began picking off bikers at the back of the pack. The downed bikes caused a jam-up as those in front tried to flee. One of the bikes began to burn as gas leaked out. The glow silhouetted the figures running up the driveway. Bullets splanged around her as someone farther down the hill found her. She looked back up the hill at Nick and nodded.

Dodging fire, they picked their way down the slope. The bikers' attention was still focused on the hill behind the house. Their approach was not noticed. Kiki stepped onto the driveway in front of the man she knew to be Gallen. The flickering firelight revealed her face, the night-vision from her helmet covering one eye.

Bullets whizzed around her as she raised her rifle. "Take off the helmet," she commanded. "I want to watch your eyes as you see this coming." First, Gallen's hands rose then dropped to the straps as he removed his helmet.

"Fucking bitch!" he screamed.

She raised the rifle. Gallen shrunk back, his hands coming up to ward off the bullet that would end his life. Behind her a bulky figure in biker cuts wearing a helmet rose, a handgun pointed at her back. She saw Gallens's eyes widen and started to turn. He fired. The large caliber bullet knocked her forward, the spray of blood coming from her chest splattered Gallen. He was a statue, unmoving, his mind trying to process what had happened.

"Go, go, go. Sean, get out of here before you get killed. I'll make sure she's dead," shouted the man.

Chapter Fifty-Six

With the yellow flames sputtering behind him, the figure stepped forward and fired a round into Russell's head.

"Sean, get out of here!" yelled the man to the frozen leader. A gunshot thundered and the man pitched to one side grabbing his throat. Blood spurted from his neck accompanied by a loud gurgling as he rolled on the ground and off the road.

Gallen spun, jumped on his bike and roared down the driveway yelling for his men to follow, pumping his fist in the air, screaming, "Ding Dong, the bitch is dead!" with a maniacal laugh.

Within seconds, the driveway was empty, except for the groaning men and bodies. The silence was broken by a scream as Tama and Joel rushed down the hill. They stood frozen staring down at the body. Behind them, one man rose from a pile of bodies at the side of the driveway and grasped Kiki's body.

Nick hugged her to him, tears flowing freely, his keening an ululating wail from his soul. Gasping for breath, Tama and OJ reached him. He enveloped Kiki's body. They stood, mouths open in shock. Nick looked at the sky, shouting until it became a sob.

Minutes, hours later he looked up. Everybody was gathered around him, speechless. Tama and OJ were sobbing. Joel's face was streaked with tears. Slowly he lifted Kiki's body. It felt so small, almost weightless, yet he staggered. They parted as he carried her to the SUV. He laid her on the deck in back, smoothing her hair from her face, arranging her arms as if she were asleep.

OJ pushed around him sobbing loudly. Nick stepped back to allow the others a moment with her. The kids gathered first. Each laid a hand on her. They were crying openly. Johnny, his face frozen, hung back as if afraid to be close.

Miriam hugged Nick as tears flowed down her cheeks.

"I'm so sorry, brother," said Stephen. "What can I do to help?"

Nick shook his head, remaining mute.

"What are you going to do with her?" asked OJ.

"I'm taking her back to her ranch. It's where she would want to be."

"You're sure?" asked Stephen.

"Yeah, it's what she told me a while back."

"No, I mean you're sure she's gone."

Nick looked at the blood-soaked body. "Her heart got blown out of her chest. Yeah, I'm sure," he sobbed.

"Do you want us to go with you?" Stephen asked.

"No, I want to be alone," Nick rasped out.

He looked at the faces around him. They were all his family. "Rosa, take care of Monique and the kids. My family will help." Miriam and Stephen nodded. "Stephen, call Brad. Johnny, call Ron. Tell him what happened. He'll let you know what's next. I'll be back." His head dropped. "I'll be back sometime."

Nick closed the back of the SUV and climbed in the driver's seat. He sat frozen, hands on the wheel, staring ahead. Johnny, Stephen and Joel dragged bikes and bodies to the side. The hostages who were alive rose, in shock, moving like zombies. Joel tapped on Nick's window when it was clear enough to pass. He eased down the driveway, seeing the sad faces as he passed.

The few miles to I-10 went quickly. "Don't you think you could stop and let me sit up front with you?" came the voice from the back. "This cow's blood is getting really sticky."

"You really want to take a chance there's not a drone overhead?"

"Maybe I'll take a nap. I sure do feel like one. Being dead has its advantages. A huge weight has been lifted off my shoulders."

"Yeah, I feel it too. Okay, we bury you at the ranch. Then what?"

"I was serious about spending time on the boat. We would be away from this world. I need that."

"Okay, I have a burner phone. Let's call Ramón. He'll have the boat ready by the time we get there. We can travel under the passports we got from Julio."

"Do you have to go back for those passports?"

"They're in my bag. I'll call Mom to tell her I'll be taking some time to get my head together."

"Better call Ron, too. He deserves to know you're going to disappear for a while."

"That may be tough. He'll try to talk me into coming back."

"That's his job," laughed Kiki. "You might be back, but not for a while."

"In the meantime, you and I have to figure out what a retired sniper who has to remain disappeared is going to do after we get tired of life on the boat again."

"That could be a really hard task. I only know what I don't want to do."

Nick punched in his friend's number in Cayman. "Ramón are you there?"

"Nick, my friend. It's been so long since I hear from you." His deep basso voice contained a smile.

"Ramón, can you ready our house?"

"Oh yes. Mon. When will you be here?"

"Two days. I'll bring my wife. Is the same housekeeping staff available?"

"Surely. Will you be landing at the private airport?"

"Sorry to disappoint you. No helicopter this time. We'll be coming in commercial."

"Rest assured, Mon, I have taken good care of your assets. Your bread has risen."

"Thank you, Ramón. We look forward to seeing you."

Chapter Fifty-Seven

It was dinner time at the mess hall after another hard day of training. Rosa and the kids looked exhausted. Johnny was beat. When his phone rang, He glanced at the number. "Blocked." *No one calls me. No one has this number.* He answered out of curiosity.

"Johnny, this is Ron Carson. Can you come in from the training site? We need to talk."

"Yeah, sure." *Ron Carson. What's he got planned?* "When?"

"Now would be nice."

"Yes, sir."

During the twenty-minute drive, his mind was in turmoil. Since the death of Kiki and the disappearance of Nick, he had continued with the training program with Rosa and the kids at the behest of Ron Carson. *Would they still be sent back to LA without Nick and Kiki? Either Ron would cancel the project or move them ahead.*

The door to the hangar was open, the blackness like a dark tunnel. He drove through, stopping so his eyes could adjust. The tap on his window startled him. Ron motioned to follow him into the belly of the C-131.

Lights came on as they went up the ramp. They entered one of the two wooden boxes inside, the only cargo in the huge hold. A gray-haired medium-height man stood, offering his hand.

"I'm David Kennedy, Director of the CIA. I've heard a lot about you."

Johnny took the hand. "Pleased to meet you." *Heard about me? I bet you know everything about me, including the color of my underwear.*

"How's the training going?" asked Kennedy.

"They're about as ready as they'll ever be without actual combat."

"Good, good," said Kennedy, rubbing his hands together. "Things are moving. We're going to kick off the return of America to California in eight weeks. As part of that, you and your troops will create as much disruption as possible."

Ron held up a hand. "The loss of Katherine Russell and Nick Sabino has been a blow to all of us. I've tried to contact Nick, but he isn't taking calls."

"We've lost all contact with him," said Kennedy. "You have any news?"

Johnny shook his head. "No, nothing. He made it clear he was leaving for a while, maybe a long while."

"We've tried to track his credit cards, phone calls, everything," said Kennedy. "He's gone. No trace."

"We did check Kiki's ranch. The place was deserted with a freshly dug grave."

The room filled with silence for a minute.

"Okay, we'll have to go without Nick," said Ron. "Talk with your team and give us an equipment list. Discuss the insertion."

"Sources tell us that Sean Gallen held his summit two weeks ago," said David Kennedy. "Julio Cardenas and his cartel have returned from Mexico and taken over southern California and Ventura. The Cs have Los Angeles and everything west and north to San Jose. The Tongs have northern California. Gallen is acknowledged as the leader. He is holding the alliance together."

"Who's planning this attack?" asked Johnny.

It's a military operation and being planned as such. We will have a teleconference in a few minutes with the president and General Edwards. Do not mention that your team has adolescents. We here at this table are the only ones who know that. The president would never approve the use of kids."

"I don't approve either, but I do understand. Kiki made it clear they were the best qualified with unique knowledge of the enemy and the territory. I still don't like it."

"Neither do we," said Ron. He punched numbers into the monitor.

"White House," answered a voice.

"Ron Carson calling for President Donaldson."

"Hold for the president."

"Ron, how are you?" came the recognizable voice of the president. "I wish to convey condolences for the death of Katherine Russell. She will be missed."

"Thank you, sir. We're doing fine, Mr. President. I'm here with David Kennedy and

Sergeant Johnny Cano. Johnny has been training a team to go into Los Angeles to create as much havoc as possible before our troops go in."

"Pleased to meet you, Johnny. I have General Edwards with me. General, explain your plan."

"Sergeant Cano, my condolences. I understand you've been training your troops in urban insurgent warfare. Is that correct?"

"Yes, sir." Johnny knew better than to volunteer more information than what was asked.

"Which areas are they familiar with?" asked the general.

"Part of my team consists of refugees from the Los Angeles and Hollywood areas, controlled by the Charon's Children. Another member is from the Ventura area, controlled by the Hijos de Hades."

"Your original mission was to recruit from the population to form a larger force," stated General Edwards. "We still want you to do that, but now with our timeframe, disruption is a priority. I realize your team is small and the extent of havoc you can create is small."

"Sir," interrupted Johnny, "we will focus on the leadership. Perhaps we should call it trickle down mayhem."

The general and the president laughed at that. "You've got the gist," said the general.

"David, where is their headquarters?" asked General Edwards.

"Gallen is still using the Los Angeles Convention Center. It is our plan to insert in the Westridge Canyonback Wilderness Park. We are familiar with it." Kennedy was careful not to say anything about it being the extraction point used before. The president didn't know about that.

"When's the kickoff?" asked President Donaldson.

"One week," said David. Ron looked at Johnny.

He had a pained expression on his face. This battle in Casa Grande had been intense but short. In LA it could go on for months and they would be on the enemy's turf. God! They needed Nick and Kiki. *I'm never ready to let go, but there's little else I have to offer them. They're certainly not kids anymore. Nice.* He nodded. Everyone on his team would be eager to avenge Kiki. Except him. He'd seen too much war.

Chapter Fifty-Eight

Newly chosen President Sean Gallen looked at the faces of his leadership team gathered around his conference table. The glass wall overlooked the main arena floor. For a few seconds he watched the men scurrying below preparing for the formal declaration of the country of Kalifornia. He'd done it. After killing that bitch Russell things had gone smoothly.

They had reached an accord as to territories and businesses. Disputes would be resolved by a council made up of these men.

"Gentlemen, thank you for helping put this together. We are adjourned until the dedication this evening. Enjoy yourselves."

As they filed out, he spoke to Julio Cardenas and Edward Ling, "A word, gents." They smiled and nodded. "Let's go to the rooftop patio. The weather is gorgeous." Sean had a shaded platform built on the roof of the arena. It provided a stunning view of the surrounding city. Cleanup efforts were proceeding, and the city was looking good, at least certain parts.

The access ladder had been replaced with a circular stairway, the hatch now a doorway. Sean waved his bodyguards back as they stood at the railing. "Two hundred years ago, the founders of California pictured this as a paradise. The climate and the resources really created an Eden. Then it got overpopulated and socialized. Today it's neither." He waved his hands across the panoramic view.

"We have the assets and we have control. Democracy doesn't work. We're not going back to a broken system. If we can resist fighting between ourselves, we'll be rich and powerful beyond our wildest dreams."

"What about the U. S. military coming back?" asked Cardenas.

"After tonight, we declare ourselves a nation and seek recognition from other countries. With that, we join the United Nations. An attack by the United States would be an invasion. The United Nations would condemn them. We could apply for military assistance."

"Mexico would recognize us quickly," said Julio. "I could see to that."

Sean's eyebrows rose at that statement. If Julio could deliver on that promise, independence was assured.

"My friends in government are still pissed about the immigration flap, talk of a wall, and tariffs." Julio smiled. "A chance to poke the elephant in the ass would be welcome. No longer an economic giant, what can the U. S. do?"

The back of Ling's head exploded. He fell backwards into a pool of blood and brains, his eyes wide and a hole in his forehead. A second later came the boom of a rifle.

Sean gaped at Ling. "No," he screamed. "I watched you die." He looked out at the city below. "You're dead!" Elbowing Julio to the floor, Sean turned to run to the doorway. Suddenly, he pitched forward. Blood and brains sprayed across the deck.

Another boom sounded. Cardenas tried to stand, but the floor was slippery with gore. As Cardenas crawled past Gallen, he looked at him. The only recognizable part was his lower jaw. Julio Cardenas ran for his life, legs sliding in the gore.

Chapter Fifty-Nine

Tama took a last look through the rifle scope. *That was for you, Kiki. Though you weren't here, you finally got the bastard.*

"Nice shooting, Tama," said Johnny. "Pack up and let's get out of here. The Cs, the Hijos and the Tong will take only minutes to figure out what's happened. They'll be after us."

Within seconds, they were mounted up. "See you at the Pt. Mugu gate." With the bikes on silent mode, they shot off in two different directions.

Tama wove a route to the west. After eight miles she turned north. She and Johnny had been on the roof of the hospital for three days. They knew the much touted announcement of a new

Kalifornia was to be made. They were waiting for the best opportunity to disrupt. Today was it.

Now they had to head to the Hijos' roadblock near Point Mugu. Joel, Rosa and Tama were setting up an attack to rescue Rosa's sister and gain some recruits. Their escape route was west to the gate, then south.

Tama marveled at the cleanup of the streets. Somewhere was a huge pile of trash.

***

From the roof of an empty office building Joel, OJ and Rosa watched the apartment complex. A busy place, it was the one where Rosa lived before she and her sister had been forced to leave and go into the mountains. That seemed like decades ago, another life.

"The woman hanging out laundry in the flowered skirt and white blouse is my other sister, Linda. She is a slave, doing housework. It is what I was forced to do until Miguel took me as a sex slave. When he tired of me, he gave me to his cousin Ricardo. I cried about my sister Monica, so Jesus took her and Arianna when we went to the mountains."

"Who is Arianna's daddy?" asked OJ.

"We will never know. Monica was passed around before she became pregnant." OJ's mouth closed as he processed this. "We can only carry three people. Linda will be one."

"Are there guards? asked Joel.

"Usually there is one. After Tama and Johnny tell us they are in place, I will go down and start an argument. When the guard comes out, OJ can take him." OJ smiled. "Then you two come in with the Kubota and the bike. From here to Point Mugu is twenty minutes. Tama and Johnny will have that opened for us."

"Rosa, can you hear me?" It was Tama on the radio. "We'll be in position at the check point in ten minutes. Call me when you're ten minutes out. We'll take care of the guards."

"Roger," responded Rosa. She looked over at Joel and OJ and got a thumbs up.

It took her five minutes to pick her way to the apartment complex yard. Nobody paid attention to her as she walked up to her sister. "Linda, get your things. We are leaving."

Her sister's mouth fell open. "I thought you were dead. Six months since the attack on Jesus and

Ricardo and we hear nothing." She threw her arms around Rosa.

"I am with the resistance. I want you to join. Pick two friends you think could fight the Hijos and have them get their things. We travel light."

"The guard will kill us."

"He will be dealt with. Now hurry."

"Only two?"

"It's all we have room for this time. We will be back. Go now." Rosa turned and hung up clothes, scanning the area, waiting.

Through their earpieces came Tama's voice. "I'm in position. Johnny's three minutes away."

Rosa clicked her radio.

Linda reappeared trailed by two other girls, barely into their teens. They carried small bundles. "This is Carmen and Juanita." Juanita's face showed bruises from a recent beating. A hoarse voice rasped from the doorway.

"What are you putas doing?" The stocky man swaggered toward them, a rifle slung on his shoulder. "Get back to work." He staggered. His hand flew to his neck as blood began to flow. He looked at the hand, not understanding what had happened.

Rosa stepped up to him, put one arm around him and shoved a knife under his ribs and into his heart with the other. The man's eyes widened. "Remember me?" she hissed. The girls were frozen. They stared, mouths agape, eyes wide. "Come. We must go," said Rosa, as she wiped the blade on the man's gang cut before she pushed him over backward. They ran for the office building.

With the bike and Kubota in silent mode, they raced away. Rosa radioed Tama, "On our way."

Chapter Sixty

Tama sighted in on the guard lounging under the umbrella as if on a picnic at the beach. His rifle was leaning against the ice chest. "You got the other one?" she whispered to Johnny. The other guard recycled his last beer into the gutter fifteen feet away, his rifle slung on his back. "Three minutes," crackled the radio in her ear. She looked at Johnny and nodded. Two shots rang out simultaneously. The two guards were on the ground. Tama watched the scene. Nothing moved.

Their vehicles stopped at the barricade. OJ stepped from the Kubota to raise it. He froze as two bikes approached. It was the next shift. The bikers saw the bodies of their companions sprawled on the ground, the bike and the Kubota idling and the boy at the barricade. Time stood still for one second. Before OJ could bring his rifle up, one biker drew a pistol and fired. The force of the shot knocked the boy backward..

Two sharp cracks rang out. The bikers were down. Joel ran to OJ. Blood seeped from his chest. "Are you hurt bad?" Unseeing eyes blinked at him. There was no comprehension in them. "We have to get out of here." OJ's eyes rolled up. Joel lifted the small body and carried it to the Kubota,

"How bad?" asked Tama over the radio.

"Chest shot. Won't know until I get a look. Lot's of blood. Where are we going?"

"Will he make the house?" Johnny asked.

Joel looked down at the blood oozing across the small bed of the Kubota. "He's bleeding out fast." From the bike, Rosa looked at OJ and Joel.

"Linda," she said over her shoulder to her sister sitting behind her, "you drive the Kubota. Joel, stay with OJ. Stop the bleeding. Carmen, you ride with me."

"I don't know how to drive that thing," wailed Linda.

"Get in. The shifter is in front of you. When you push the pedal, it goes. When you take your foot off, it stops. We'll start slow. We have to get out of here. There may be more Hijos coming."

"Johnny and I will take the Hijos guards at the entrance to Point Mugu," said Tama. "Mugu has first aid and a medivac. I'll tell them we're coming. Joel, you get on the radio and explain OJ's injuries. I want them prepped when we arrive."

"Roger," responded Joel.

Rosa had studied the maps and led them west toward Point Mugu. "Carmen, watch Linda. If she has trouble let me know so I can stop."

They started slowly, but the ATV was easy to drive. Linda caught on fast. Ten minutes later, they approached the Hijos barricade. Three guards were sprawled on the ground, pools of blood spreading across the asphalt. The Marine guards had the gate pulled back. A Humvee off to one side signaled for them to follow. They flew through as Tama and Johnny followed. The medevac was already running, rotors spinning up. Two medics waited with a stretcher. Gently, they lifted the limp body onto it.

"Joel," said Tama, "you go with OJ. We're going to the house but we'll be in radio contract." Joel climbed aboard. Within seconds the helicopter lifted off. They waved, but Joel was intent on OJ, watching the medics struggle to save his life.

Rosa had huge tears rolling down her cheeks. She should have been ready for trouble. She should have given him cover. Her misery was interrupted by Tama.

"We need to get to the house before this place is swarming with Hijos. Who are our recruits?"

Rosa pointed to the tallest of the three girls. "This is Linda, my sister. Her friends Carmen and Juanita came with us." The two girls nodded. Nobody was smiling.

"I'm Tama and this is Johnny. Let me check to see if our route is clear."

She switched channels. "Ron, have you been monitoring us?"

"Yeah, we have eyes overhead. Your party at the Cs headquarters has stirred up a mess. Nobody's in charge, so people are running around everywhere. So far, there's no organized search for you. The streets from the Mugu gate south and east are clear. The Hijos are discovering they've been attacked and are more organized. There's a pack of twelve heading toward you. You could stay at Mugu."

"That would mean we'd have to reinsert. It'll set us back."

"Get moving. I put them fifteen minutes out."

"That's fifteen minutes from the barricade. It'll take them a while to organize a search from there," said Tama. "Keep us informed of trouble."

"Roger," responded Ron.

Tama turned to her group. "We need to get moving. Linda, you drive the ATV." She handed Linda OJ's headset. "Johnny will lead. Rosa will stay close to you. I'll follow to see no trouble comes up from behind. If you have any problems, sing out." She left no room for discussion. Before now, the leadership role was not firm. Tama stepped up as if born to the position.

Chapter Sixty-One

The house they'd stayed in after rescuing Kiki was their headquarters. The solar plant supplied power, the swimming pool still had plenty of water. The house was close to the storeroom at the Mormon Church, so food and medical supplies weren't a problem. The school across the street became the housing and training center for their recruits.

Gathered around the table in the cafeteria at the school, Tama addressed the group. "OJ didn't make it." Her voice cracked as she delivered the news. Rosa broke down, hands covering her face, her body wracked with sobs.

A visibly shaken Johnny Cano stood up. "There…there was nothing anybody could have done." After taking a deep breath, he continued.

"OJ was a good soldier, dedicated to freeing California from the Cs. He was a causality of war. It's what happens. What we do from here is critical." Johnny looked from face to face. "We have a job to do. More of us may get hurt or worse. We honor OJ's memory by continuing the fight."

Tama raised her head. Her expression went from grief stricken to hard. "We struck a blow today against the Cs, the Hijos and the formation of a new state. The U. S. is coming back and it's not someday but soon. This dream of a new country won't come together in time with the loss of their leaders. We have to keep them busy defending themselves. So, time for formal introductions. I'm Tama. This is Johnny," she said, putting her hand on his shoulder. "He is our drill instructor."

She sighed, a little lost for words. "Some history. Six months ago, Joel, OJ and I were scavenging, hiding out from the Cs and trying to stay alive." She paused at the mention of OJ. "A change literally dropped into our lives when Kiki Russell parachuted into our midst after killing a bunch of Cs. She was injured, needing help to get away from the hunting party. We brought her here, and that's how we met her partner, Nick. With

Nick's leadership, we escaped Los Angeles met Rosa and her sister Monica on the way."

She looked at Rosa. "We used to be a bunch of kids. Rosa helped us to grow up. She's like our mother/older sister now. Time for you girls to grow up. If you join us, you won't be victims anymore."

Chapter Sixty-Two

Two years later

Nick hung onto the wheel as the trimaran heeled, lifting one hull from the water. The wind had freshened as the sun was setting, and they were skimming across the blue Pacific. Kiki held him from behind, her chin resting on his shoulder. "Where we going, Captain?"

They were heading north, no land in sight. "Nowhere in particular, just sailing. We left the U. S. two years and twenty-three days ago, but who's counting. Are you bored with life at sea yet? "

"I'm not there, but I can see it coming."

"How about new scenery?" Nick looked back at her.

"Whatcha got in mind?

"Our trip through the Panama Canal was interesting, but blue water is the same here as in the Caribbean. Want to spend a little time ashore, maybe Matazalán?"

"How about Acapulco? I always wanted to dive off those cliffs."

"K, that's not going to happen."

"Party pooper." She was getting bored.

"It's time for my monthly call to Stephen. Take the wheel. I'll be back shortly."

"Aye aye, Captain,"

In the main cabin, Nick turned on the running-lights and checked the radar. No storms in sight. Good. He opened a shortwave channel. "CQ CQ. Stephen are you there? Over."

"Hey, Nick. We've been waiting for your call. I've got some bad news. Mom took a fall, broke her hip. She's in the hospital now. Surgery is scheduled in two days. She's asking after you. Over."

Nick flinched at the news. From his time with his dad, he knew elderly people started the clock ticking seriously after a hip break. A five-year lifespan was average, but a year or two was not uncommon. He'd seen it. A lot depended on their attitude. Some gave up during the rehab, finding it too difficult. Once bedridden, the trolley would race downhill. Others with something to recover for came back well.

"How's she taking it? Over."

"Her mood is generally good, but occasionally she says things like 'Well, I am old.' Any chance you can come back? It would lift her spirits. Over."

"I will return, but it may take me a week. Tell her. Over."

"Yeah, it'll give her something to look forward to. Say, Ron Carson's called twice. You should give him a call. Over."

"Thanks, Stephen. Look after Mom. I'll see you in about a week. Over and out." *Ron Carson. What does he want? Do I want to find out?* He climbed back up on deck and stepped behind Kiki, cradling her.

"Everything all right?" she asked.

"Mom broke her hip. I need to go see her. How about we sail to Puerto Peñasco instead of Acapulco? I can catch a shuttle from there."

"Yeah, I could knock around the city for a while. Not many cartel people there, but I'll bleach my hair, put a huge black mole on my chin. Nobody will recognize me."

Nick laughed at the image in his mind. "Ron Carson called. Think I should call him back?"

Kiki shrugged. "Let's find out what he has to say."

Nick returned below deck and got Stephen back. "Stephen, could you put me on a phone-patch to Ron Carson? Over." *Am I doing the right thing? Kiki and I left that world. Kiki's life depends on her remaining dead.*

"Yeah. It'll take me a couple of minutes to set it up. Hold on. Over."

"Hello, Nick. Are you there?"

Nick recognized Ron's voice. "I'm here, Ron. Tell me how things are there. I haven't listened to any news from the U. S. in quite a while."

"Out of the country, huh? How are you doing?"

"I'm getting along. Stephen and I talk once in a while, but I'm still recovering."

"Things are nearly back to normal here, though with a lot fewer people. We took California back, thanks in no small part to you and K… Sorry, didn't want to bring her up. It's probably still painful. Your team made a real difference. Once Sean Gallen was dead, the gangs were headless. Nobody could pull their coalition together. The

Mexican cartel fled back across the border, The Charon's Children is about gone. Most of the members are dead or in jail."

"That's good news." Nick smiled to himself. *Things had moved fast. Did that mean that their enemies were gone?*

"You haven't heard, but Oliver–OJ–was killed in the fight. He was awarded the Congressional Gold Medal."

"OJ! Shit." Nick felt his throat choke up. "Are the other kids and Rosa okay?"

"Yeah. They stayed in LA helping to pull everything together. The president would like to award you a medal for all you've done. Will we get a chance to meet with you?"

Nick stopped. *Sure I'll be back in the U. S., but do I want to see these people again? I do miss home and family and the life of being an expat is getting old. What about Kiki?* He realized that his initial idea of a short visit was not realistic. "Let me think about it. I'll call you in a few days."

"Thanks for speaking with me, Nick. It's good to hear your voice."

"Nice talking to you, too." He sat unmoving for a few minutes. Telling Kiki about OJ would tear her up. It had to be done. He went up on deck.

"Well, how's Ron doing?"

"He seemed fine. The country's nearly back to normal–at least a close as we can be with the losses we've suffered."

"Wow. I thought it would take years." Kiki smiled.

"OJ got killed in the battle for Los Angeles."

Kiki froze. The only sound was the slap of the waves and the hum of the wind through the rigging. Nick put his arms around her.

Mechanically, she steered the boat. The phosphorescent algae created a glowing trail behind them showing where they'd been. Ahead it was dark. At last she turned to him. Starlit tears glistened on her cheeks. She hugged Nick tightly. "Why does my family always have to die?"

Chapter Sixty-Three

As Nick and Kiki sailed into the Sea of Cortez, they passed a freighter chugging along flying Venezuelan colors. The shallow draft of their trimaran gave them more freedom to maneuver and the wind from the west was steady and strong. This heading would take them all the way into Puerto Peñasco by mid-afternoon. Kiki radioed ahead, arranging for a berth. Nearing the marina, they furled the sails and motored in. Other pleasure craft were there, so they went unnoticed.

"Let's get margaritas on the Malicón," said Kiki. "I have a powerful thirst."

"I could use a shrimp cocktail, too," said Nick. "Let's go to Flavio's."

They walked into the open air deck overlooking the bay. The restaurant was crowded. One woman sat alone at a table staring at the bay, some documents on the table in front of her. She looked American with dark hair and a pretty face.

"Excuse me," said Kiki. "Would you mind if we joined you? The other tables are taken."

"Please do." She gestured to the empty chairs.

Nick reached across the table. I'm Rick Robinson. This is Kathy, my wife."

"Carol Goldman," said the woman, shaking Nick's hand first. Kiki stood and reached across the table for her hand. "Are you touristing?"

"Sort of," said Nick. "We sailed in on that trimaran about an hour ago." He pointed to their docked boat. "Been at sea for a while and wanted margaritas, shrimp and land under our feet."

"Where did you sail from?" asked Carol.

Innocent enough question, thought Kiki, glancing at the documents. "We left Corpus Christi a while back. Came through the canal a couple of weeks ago and been moving up the west coast," Kiki lied.

"Carol, you're not dressed like the typical Puerto Peñasco tourist," commented Kiki, observing her casual business attire.

"I'm acting as point person for a project near Tucson. We're moving, and some of the equipment is large. Rather than try to get it permitted for overland transport, we're going by ship. It's easier."

Kiki watched the woman during her explanation. Though plausible, her body language said it was not quite true, certainly not the entire story.

"I'm a little familiar with Tucson," said Nick. "What kind of business does your company do?"

"We're an obscure genetic research laboratory," said Carol. "So, you've been to Tucson. Any plans to return?"

Nice subject change, observed Kiki.

"I've got some business in Phoenix that requires my presence. I anticipate a short visit before resuming our voyage. Kathy and I want to travel up the west coast to Vancouver before returning to the real world."

Carol turned to Kiki. "Are you going to Phoenix, too?"

She shrugged. "I'm not needed, and there're things we need for the boat. I'm going to knock around here for a day or so. Rick's business shouldn't take long."

"I've been here for a while arranging everything for the shipping."

There was sadness in her body language and tone of voice. Something more was going on, thought Kiki. "You're on your own?"

"Our freighter is due in tomorrow, so I'll be overseeing the lading of equipment," she said, not answering Kiki's question. "Actually, I'm enjoying your American company. My people will be arriving soon."

The freighter they passed earlier, thought Kiki. *Venezuelan registry was interesting.* "If there's anything I can do to help, let me know. Once I get our boat restocked and cleaned up, I won't have a lot to do."

"That would be nice. I'd like that. During my time here, I've found the good restaurants and the not so good. Maybe we can have dinner tomorrow. I may bring a few people along."

"That would be nice," said Kiki. The bill of lading Kiki saw listed Kihhim as the shipper. Strange name. People and equipment boarding a ship in an obscure port like Puerto Peñasco? She would check out Kihhim tonight. Was it a front for those searching for her?

Chapter Sixty-Four

Nick walked into Stephen's restaurant *Cocina de Sabino* at three-o'clock. When Barb, Stephen's wife saw him, she gasped, then ran over and gave him a hug.

"Oh, Nick. It is so good to have you here."

"Hi, Barb. Is Stephen here?"

"He's at the hospital."

"How's Mom?"

"She'll be better when she sees you." Barb put her hand on Nick's arm. "How are you doing?"

"I'm doing fine. It's nice to be back. Your family doing okay?"

"We are. Life is getting back to the new normal. Business is good, kids in school. Stephen and I are working harder than ever."

"I'll go on over to the hospital. See you for dinner?"

"Only if you eat here," she laughed.

Nick tapped on the doorframe as he peeked into Miriam's room. "Hi, Mom."

Her eyes lit up. "Oh, Nick, I was praying you'd come. I'm so glad you're here." Tears filled her eyes.

Nick gave her a hug. She seemed frail. "You look pretty good, Mom," he fibbed. "I'm here to whip you through therapy and get you back on your feet. How's it going?"

"It hurts, gosh darn it. I'll get better if for no other reason than I want to go to the bathroom by myself."

They laughed. Stephen rose and gave Nick a hug. "Glad you're here. Are you back, brother?"

Nick shrugged. He really didn't know yet.

His mother cranked the bed up more. "How are you doing, Nick?"

"Fine, Mom. I'm past the worst." Nick lied. *I want to tell them that Kiki is fine, but not yet.*

"Tell me what you've been doing," said Miriam.

For the next hour Nick told them of sailing around the Caribbean and the Panama Canal. Miriam shook her head at the idea of Nick just sailing around aimlessly.

An older woman with a drill instructor look came in. "Time for therapy, Mrs. Sabino. You young gentlemen are welcome to come back later."

Nick liked her take-charge attitude.

At Nick's rented car he turned to Stephen. "I'm going up to the house. It's time to call Ron again. I'll go visit Mom and meet you at the restaurant in a few hours." They hugged again.

"Ron Carson," said the voice.

"Hi, Ron. Nick here."

"Nick! Good to hear your voice again. How are you getting along?"

"I'm fine, back in the U. S." *There, he said it. Now Ron knew.*

"That's great. Can we get together? I want to bring you up to date."

"Sure. How about a trip to Arizona? I'm here because of Mom. She had a partial hip replacement." *I don't want to travel anywhere publically yet.*

"How's she doing?"

"Her spirits seem good, and the rehab's going well. Her therapist reminds me of Johnny the drill instructor. Mom won't get to slack off."

"I can catch a hop to Pinal Air Park tomorrow. You want to come there?"

"Two days would be better. I have things to do and I want to spend time with Mom."

"Okay, sure. I understand. I'll come to Casa Grande in a couple of days. I'd like to see your mom, wish her well."

"That would be great. I know she'd like to see you." *It might be the boost to really get her moving.*

"The president would like to give you an award for your service."

"I'm not ready for that kind of exposure, yet, don't want to bring attention to myself."

"I understand, though we're positive you're safe."

"See you in a couple of days, Ron." *He seemed so sure. Maybe they could return to his family.*

Nick called Kiki. "Hey, Babe"

"Hi, Nick. How's your mom?" "She's about as expected. I think she'll have an easy recovery. Stephen and his family are doing well. Actually, things in Casa Grande are good. What have you been up to?"

"I did some online searching on Kihhim, you know, Carol's company. Did you know Kihhim is Tohono O'Odham for the village? It's a very interesting story. Take a look."

"How did you know the name?"

"It was on the bill of lading she had."

"Oh. I'll look it up tonight. I'm going to come down tomorrow."

"Why?"

"For you, of course."

"Right. What's the real reason?"

"I'll tell you more tomorrow morning. See you then."

"If I'm not on the boat, I'll be on the dock helping Carol. I like her. She's hiding some things, but it has nothing to do with us, I'm sure. A lot of her people are coming in. Interesting group."

Nick needed to think. He wanted Kiki to return from Rocky Point with him. He had to have assurances they and their families would be safe. While his mind turned over the issue, he did a search on Kihhim.

The media articles talked about it as an isolated community at the foot of Baboquivari Peak, a Native American holy mountain near the town of Sells. They had been obscure until they were accused of potential terrorism. *Potential terrorism? What's that? Some would consider Kiki and him potential terrorists.* He watched a television clip of Kihhim. Sure there was paranoia in the U. S. after the bio attack, but Nick couldn't see where these people could be terrorists. He and Kiki had dealt with real terrorists. The only thing Kihhim seemed fanatical about was being left alone. He logged off. It was time to visit Mom again and go to dinner. Was it really safe? God, he hoped so. How would Kiki react to the idea of coming back? It would be her ass on the line. What if she said no?

Chapter Sixty-Five

"K," Nick called. Their boat was empty. The dock was full with people getting ferried out to the freighter, men, women, families. He found Kiki in cutoff jeans and a tee shirt standing next to Carol in a small group. She introduced him to Jamie Wong, a short roundish man with intense eyes. Next to Wong was Adriana Getzwiller, a tall stout woman in tan slacks and white shirt. She left to help load an older woman in a wheelchair onto the next boat. "This looks like quite an operation," said Nick.

"We have to leave," said Jamie, frowning. "It's not safe for us here any longer." With sadness in his eyes, he looked at Nick.

We've had to do the same, thought Nick. He gave Kiki's hand a squeeze. "Anything we can do to help?"

"Don't say anything to anybody, Rick," said Carol. "Nobody can know. By high tide tomorrow afternoon, we'll be gone."

As Nick pulled Kiki away, he said over his shoulder, "You know where our boat is. You need any help, just ask."

"Thank you," said Carol, looking harried.

"We need to talk," whispered Nick as they walked away.

Back on the boat, he sat across from her at the table. "I'm meeting with Ron Carson tomorrow. I want you to come back with me." He expected a shocked look. Instead, she smiled.

"I thought this was coming, and I want it, too. We need assurances my resurrection won't endanger anyone. Ron will sell us a good line, but in the end we have to believe."

"Yeah." He smiled. He had anticipated an argument. She knew him well.

"I did what you said and looked up Kihhim. It's quite a story. Is it the paranoia of the U. S. that has the government after them?"

"Carol opened up to me last night. I think she had to let this out. They're running. Kihhim does very advanced genetic development. It's their technology everybody is after. Kihhim doesn't want to let go, afraid it would be misused. They don't want to work for anybody either."

"That's what I got out of the stories I read. Where can they go?"

"Carol said nothing when I asked. I don't blame her. If it's not some government after them, it's a corporation. Religious fanatics have begun a crusade against Kihhim. They have no shortage of enemies."

Kiki picked up her phone, punching in a number. "Carol, need a break? Would you and any others want another dinner tonight? We'll buy. Okay, we'll pick you up at eight. How about El Capitán? See you."

Nick nodded. "Good idea."

Four of them sat the table gazing over the bay spread out below. The freighter lay offshore, its lights dancing across the water. On the dock, people were still lined up, shuffling to the small boats.

Kiki held up her margarita for a toast. "Here's to the best for you and your group." Their glasses clinked.

"Carol, Jamie, I looked online and read the media story of Kihhim," said Kiki.

Jamie and Carol glanced at each other.

"I saw the name on your paperwork," explained Kiki.

"I'm sorry you are being treated this way," said Nick. "Rest assured we will do nothing to compromise you."

Kiki rested her hand on top of Carol's. "Rick and I had to flee the United States. People were after us, some of them in the government, so we understand."

Carol's eyes widened, Jamie Wong's gaze moved between Nick and Kiki. "We've never done anything like this," Carol said. "As soon as John, Katharine and Leticia get here, we'll leave."

"The only advice I have," offered Nick, "is don't delay."

"Yeah," added Kiki, "and be careful where you go. Bad as the U. S. is at times, most other places in the world are worse."

Their food arrived–beautiful plates, delicious aromas. They ate in silence. Nick watched Jamie and Carol. They were leaving their homes, perhaps forever. He knew the ache that caused.

Back at the dock Carol gave Nick and Kiki hugs, Jamie shook hands with each. "Perhaps we'll meet again," he said.

"Perhaps so," said Nick. He and Kiki waved as they boarded a boat to go out to the ship.

Nick held Kiki's hand as she stepped onto their trimaran. He pulled her into a tender embrace. "I'd be lost without you," he whispered into her ear as he nuzzled.

"You wouldn't be in all this trouble if it weren't for me."

He kissed her tenderly. "I wouldn't have it any other way."

They moved toward the forward berth, shedding clothes. Nick pushed her onto the bunk, leaned over her and kissed her deeply. Arms around his neck, she pulled him to her. When at last their lips parted, Nick kissed her neck. She sighed as his lips continued downward hardening her nipples, causing her to shiver.

Their lovemaking was intense, each doing for the other. Their orgasms were an explosive climax. The tension streamed out like water from a ruptured dam.

Kiki awoke to the throb of an engine. Donning a tee shirt, she climbed on deck. The lights of the freighter were moving. *What happened? They were supposed to leave in the afternoon. Had something gone wrong?* She watched until Nick joined her, he too, awakened by the deep beat of the engines.

"Something changed," said Nick. "We can only hope it's not too bad."

Chapter Sixty-Six

From the Chuichu highway Nick called Stephen at the rebuilt *Cocina de Sabino* restaurant. "We'll be in town before three. Can you arrange for food delivery from the restaurant? We're going to have some company tonight."

"Good idea eating at the house. Mom has been booted from her hospital room. They claimed she needed to go home. Her drill sergeant therapist will be there until I arrive and every day until she's walking. How many for dinner?"

Nick counted in his head. "Six adults."

"I'll bring the banquet-size meal. You can eat leftovers. Mom won't be up, and I've tasted your cooking. See you at six-thirty."

Nick pulled up to the front door, parking next to an unknown car. "Must be the therapist," he said to Kiki. As they entered, he called, "Mom I'm home. Got a surprise for you."

"It better be a good one," she called from her bedroom. "Nurse Ratchet took her training at the SS school of interrogation and physical therapy. I need a break."

Nick led Kiki down the hall. He peered in. His mom was in her wheelchair, the therapist hovering to one side. Beads of sweat glistened on Miriam's forehead. She'd been working.

"Nick, I'm glad you're here so this woman can leave. She's killing me. What's my surprise? Did you bring me chocolates?"

"Better, much better." He pulled Kiki into the room.

Nick thought Miriam was having a heart attack. Her face paled and she gasped for breath.

Kiki wrapped her arms around Miriam. "I'm real, not a ghost."

Great sobs came from Miriam as she pulled Kiki to her. "How?" she asked in a muffled voice.

"Long story, Mom," said Kiki. "I'm here now. I'll go through the whole story at dinner."

"Dinner! Who's going to cook? Not Nick, I hope." They all laughed. "Help get me dressed, please," she said to the therapist. "What's that noise?" There was a thumping outside. "Is that one of those helicopters?"

"Yeah, Mom. Ron Carson wanted to drop in for dinner and to wish you a big get well. I'll get the door."

Nick opened the door to find two suited men with MP 5 submachine guns. "Secret Service," said one. He went inside. Nobody moved. Within five minutes he was back. "Clear."

Ron Carson, wearing casual slacks and an open-necked sport shirt emerged from the helicopter, turned and steadied another similarly dressed man stepping out. President Jack Donaldson waved at him. *HOLY SHIT!*

"Hope you don't mind my coming unannounced," the president said. "Sometimes I have to escape and do something that is actually good. Nobody knows I'm here, so let's not alert the media."

Nick laughed. "It's a pleasure finally meeting you face-to-face, Mr. President." He shook the president's hand and turned to Ron. "It's good to see you again." He held onto Ron's hand for a few seconds. "I have a little confession for you, too. Let's go see Mom." He turned to lead the men inside.

"Mom, I have another surprise for you," he called out.

The astonished looks on the three faces in the bedroom were only matched by those on Ron Carson's and the president's faces at seeing Kiki. Ron lowered his head and shook it. "Of course," he muttered. "It had to be."

"Mrs. Sabino, how are you doing?" asked the president.

"Well, now that I'm getting my heart under control, I'm doing better. I'd bow but my therapist won't let me."

"Hey," called Stephen's voice from the hallway, "whose chariot is that parked in the driveway. I have dinner." He walked into the already crowded bedroom. His mouth dropped as he saw Donaldson.

"I'm Jack Donaldson," the president said, holding out his hand.

"Stephen Sabino," Nick's brother stuttered.

His two boys peeked around the doorway. "Aunt Kiki!" they yelled. Stephen looked at her and whitened.

"Let's go into the den where we have more room," said Nick.

The line of people filed out and down the hallway. "Who's that?" whispered Stephen's youngest. "Is he important?"

"He must be," said the other. "He gets to ride in a helicopter."

"Drinks, anyone?" asked Barb from the bar. Her mouth fell open as she saw the president. When she looked at Kiki, a glass fell from her hand, shattering on the tile floor. "Kiki, you're…you're alive." she stammered.

"Let me help with that," said Kiki, bending to pick up the shards. Barb was frozen.

"I'm Jack Donaldson," the president said, walking toward her. "What do you recommend to drink?"

Barb recovered. "We brought Mexican food. How about margaritas?"

"That's fine," said the president.

Yesses echoed around the room. "Nick, would you help me put another leaf in the table?" asked

Stephen. "And I need help getting the food out of the truck, too."

"Katharine and I can get the table," said Ron, moving toward it.

"I feel so helpless," said Miriam.

"You can keep me entertained," said the president. He pulled a chair over to her. Within minutes, they were in deep conversation.

As Nick and Stephen lowered the ramp from the catering van, Stephen hissed, "You didn't tell me Ron Carson and the president were coming. And Kiki! How…"

"I'll tell the story when everybody's together."

Chapter Sixty-Seven

The plates were cleared, coffee served. Ron glanced around the table. "Okay, Nick, Katharine, what happened?"

Kiki let out a long breath. "With the Charon's Children and the Hijos de Hades offering bounties for my head, the only way to keep my friends and family safe was to die. Nick and I staged it."

"Ms. Russell," said the president, "you remind me of my cat Snurffles. He's used eight of his lives and is still getting white hair all over my suits. Drives my dry cleaner nuts."

She laughed before continuing, "The biggest danger was if Nick got shot by one of our own snipers."

"I did get shot, but the body armor stopped the slug. Hurt like hell," said Nick.

"What about all the blood?" asked Stephen. "Kiki was covered. Her guts sprayed out all over Sean Gallen."

"Fake," she said. "Gallen had to believe. That's why the *coup de gras* to the back of my head. He could have no doubt I was dead."

"Kiki was gone, but I had to disappear," said Nick. "We left the country."

"Where?" asked Ron.

"The Caribbean most of the time," Kiki said.

"Will you give me lessons in that disappearing thing?" joked the president. "If I read the reports correctly, that was the second time you died. There are times I feel like I need to get away."

"You're going to run for office again?" asked Miriam.

"Ma'am, I am looking forward to a much less tumultuous second term." He let out a sigh. "This meal is one of the few breaks without an agenda. Well, it actually does have an agenda. I only learned the full story of the missions that Nick and Katherine did after we had retaken California."

He stood and walked around the table to Nick. From his pocket he withdrew a large gold medal. "Nicholas Sabino, from a grateful nation who will never know the whole story, thank you." He walked to Kiki. "Ms. Katherine Russell Sabino, I believe this is a true first. Neither I nor any previous president has ever had a greater pleasure than awarding a posthumous Congressional Medal to the actual recipient. Thank you."

There was a smattering of applause. Ron Carson rose. "I wish to thank both of you and your family. The battle of the Sabino is one to remember. Nick, Katherine, I want to fill you in completely on what followed. Mr. President, I'm not sure you should hear this."

"I have things to do in the chopper. Come get me before you're ready to leave." He walked away trailed by the two Secret Service men.

Ron sat down. "The kids and woman you rescued from Los Angles became soldiers. You understood that was against my wishes, but I came to realize as did you that there was no other way. It saved a lot of lives. That small force went back into Los Angeles and broke apart the coalition Sean Gallen had formed. The Charon's Children were leaderless as was the Tong in northern California. More importantly, they left Julio Cardenas alive with the absolute belief that *La Diabla* had risen from the dead and returned. He fled the U. S. Your threat of hunting him down if he ever returned burned into his mind."

"Where are the kids today?" asked Miriam.

"Tama is in the U. S. Army." Kiki sucked in a breath. "Joel also is in the Army as a medic. Rosa is running a rehabilitation center for the women who had been held by the gangs. Johnny is back here with the Sheriff's department. OJ was buried with full honors."

There was a gasp from Miriam. "OJ was killed?"

"Yes, ma'am, I'm sorry to say. His death tore Joel up pretty badly. It pushed Joel to become a medic. It hardened Tama like tempered steel."

Nick looked at Kiki. Her face was a frozen mask.

"Nick, Kiki, what are you going to do now?" asked Ron.

"I want to go to medical school," said Nick. "I'd like to come back here to practice."

"If the president or I can help, contact me," said Ron. "And you Katherine. What are your plans?"

"I'll let you know when I figure it out."

"Stay in touch, both of you. I mean that. I'll go get the president so he can say his goodbyes."

The president entered with Ron. "I want to thank you again for your service. Ms. Sabino, thank you for hosting us tired old politicos. Let us know if you need anything." The thudding of the helicopter signaled his departure.

That night Nick and Kiki lay beside each other, silent, bodies touching. Nick's soft snoring comforted her, but she couldn't sleep. The familiar tingling started in her mind, but she pushed it back. Keeping the Director away was something she hadn't been able to do before. *Was she changing? Perhaps.*

A nagging question would not go away. *What does a sniper, one truly in the Zen of that profession do in retirement?*

For a sample of *Risen from the Dead,* the sequel to *Dead Again* and the next book in the Dead Series flip the page.

RISEN FROM THE DEAD

Prologue

"Very soon, I will be killed by our enemies." The soft brown eyes of the white-robed man looked at his twenty followers. Although his face was gentle, radiating peace, his steely voice bit into Mohammed al Jar's soul as he continued. "I have foreseen that my time has come. Do not lament or wail. Allah will provide us with better weapons to strike fear into the hearts of millions and decimate our foes."

Mohammed's chest swelled. The forces of the Great Satan pursue us on the ground, kill us from the air until only the stoutest of heart remain. I and my brothers will do whatever this man counsels, gladly martyring ourselves for Allah.

"You will travel to meet a powerful Imam who will sacrifice himself for Allah and our fight." Holding up a jeweled knife, he said to me, "Mohammed, use this sacred knife to martyr this Imam as he goes to meet Allah in the next life." He handed the knife to Mohammed. "Each of you will taste his blood, for it is holy. You will share his last breath, for it will change you into powerful weapons to destroy our enemies. You will attack our enemies in their own lands killing thousands of infidels. This I have foreseen."